ENDORSEMENTS FOR
THE LEGACY OF LORD BADEN-POWELL

"Eleanor Clark magically weaves the story of Lord Baden-Powell's life and Scouting's values into a tale of today's youth in Scouting. It is a must read for the youth of today and tomorrow. Parents considering whether or not to choose Boy Scouts for their child would greatly benefit from reading this terrific book."

Glenn A. Adams
President, National Eagle Scout Association (NESA)
Eagle Scout Class of 1973

"Eleanor Clark brings to life Scouting as an adventure, building skill and character for a new generation. As an Eagle Scout, I give two thumbs up for this inspiring tale!"

Rick Perry
Governor of Texas
Eagle Scout Class of 1964

"Through Lord Baden-Powell's time-honored traditions, Eleanor Clark captures the excitement, challenge, and skill sets of Scouting in this riveting story. A great read for Scouts and families from all walks of life!"

Pete Sessions
Member of Congress (TX-32)
Eagle Scout Class of 1970

"For more than a century, Scouting has shaped the lives of young people around the world through the important values it upholds and impacts. Eleanor Clark's book captures the essence of Scouting while recalling its beginnings through the character of its visionary founder. Young people everywhere will enjoy this educational and inspirational book."

Rex W. Tillerson
Chairman and CEO, Exxon Mobil Corporation
Eagle Scout Class of 1965

YOUNG MEN OF HONOR SERIES | BOOK I

THE LEGACY OF
LORD BADEN-POWELL

FATHER OF SCOUTING

HONORING THE BOY SCOUTS OF AMERICA'S 100TH ANNIVERSARY

ELEANOR CLARK

WinePress **WP** Publishing

WinePress Publishing (PO Box 428, Enumclaw, WA 98022) functions only as book publisher. As such, the ultimate design, content, editorial accuracy, and views expressed or implied in this work are those of the author.

ISBN 13: 978-1-57921-987-1
ISBN 10: 1-57921-987-X
Library of Congress Catalog Card Number: 2008934801

Printed in China.

APC-FT041801

DEDICATION

In memory of Lord Baden-Powell, Chief Scout of the World, and whose life sparked my imagination to write a book about his legacy.

To the Differently-abled Boy Scouts, who work so hard to achieve their badges.

To the Boy Scouts who shared timeless stories with me.

I hope you discover many great adventures through the pages of this work of fiction honoring the Boy Scouts of America's 100th anniversary. May you continue to be young men of honor.

Thank you for an exciting journey!

CONTENTS

ACKNOWLEDGMENTS

To my Lord and Savior, Jesus Christ, who has blessed me with the greatest family, life, and country. May every word bring honor and glory to Your name.

To my children, grandchildren, and great-grandchildren, who learned early in life the values of Scouting.

To my professor, Keith Whitaker, a Scout who encouraged me to write and taught me how to express my thoughts and feelings in print.

To my team of writers and editors, who understood my passion for Scouting and breathed life into my Scout stories with the skill of their pens.

ACKNOWLEDGEMENTS

CHAPTER ONE

THE UNWRITTEN CODE

John drifted in and out of his groggy state. *Am I asleep or awake?* Consciousness toyed with the edges of his mind.

He didn't want to wake up but he knew that soon the bugle would blow, calling the members of his Scout troop to assembly before breakfast. Still, he fought against opening his eyes. But then another force made its presence known, a pressure deep within him that he knew he would soon have to give in and answer. He sighed, threw back the edge of his bedroll, and sat up.

The world gave a crazy rock and roll.

John's eyes popped open, and his not-fully-awake mind scrambled to make sense of what was happening. Before he could focus, he felt himself falling . . . falling . . .

This can't be!

He plunged into darkness, his mind further rebelling. He couldn't breathe. A spark of reason on the edge of his

1

brain told him he was in water, and he fought to get to the surface.

Emerging from the cold, murky world, he sputtered and coughed as he began to tread water. Then he heard . . . heard what? Laughing?

Confusion was slowly replaced by anger as John came fully awake. He was in the lake! Several boys in canoes surrounded him. Someone had placed him—cot and all—adrift in the lake, and now they were watching him.

"You've got to be kidding me!" John's yell could probably be heard all the way to the front gate. "You guys are gonna get it. Just wait and see."

One of the favorite, although unauthorized, activities at Boy Scout camp was playing pranks on one another. This year, John had clearly been winning that particular contest—until this morning. But he could take it as well as give it, and his anger faded as he joined in the laughter.

One of the nearby canoes held three cackling boys—Ben, Philip, and Preston. John knew them to be the primary instigators and most likely the architects of his disaster. He swam over to their boat.

"Good one, guys." He forced a cheerfulness he didn't entirely feel. "Must've been hard to carry my cot down, get me loaded in the canoe, and push me off—without waking me up."

"Not so hard." John watched Philip try to hold back his mirth, but he failed and a laugh burst forth. "You sleep like a rock."

That confirmed it. They had thought it out carefully, but not carefully enough.

Across from him, his friends Samuel and Jacob had captured his canoe and were retrieving his cot and his gear. *Good.* That only left John with one task.

Scouts are taught how to get out of the water and into a boat that can turn over easier than any other watercraft. The boys in the canoe must offset a Scout's weight as he quickly stretches himself up and across the edge to grab the other side. Then, ever so slowly, he has to pull himself into the boat as the others continue to counterbalance his weight. *Slow* is the operational word. *Sudden* is not a word that goes well with canoes.

They had practiced this drill over and over.

Holding onto the side of the boat, John reached up to shake Philip's hand. "Beautifully executed prank, man."

Philip grinned and reached for his hand. "Well, I'm surprised you—"

John didn't shake the hand. Instead he pushed off the side of the canoe with his legs, drawing Philip into the water after him and overturning the canoe. All three boys splashed into the drink.

Nope, they hadn't thought it through far enough.

Angry voices shouted behind him as John swam to the canoe containing his gear. Samuel and Jacob had folded his cot, making room for him. John made short work of climbing into the craft. He picked up a paddle and backed the canoe away from Philip as the boy started to swim toward him. "The mark of a master prankster"—he smiled as he pulled out of reach—"is to have the presence of mind to turn a stunt around when someone pulls one on you. But I'm not going to let you swim over here and reverse it *again.*" His laugh drifted across the surface of the lake.

Philip scowled then swam back to help his friends right their canoe. Another thing they had been taught was how to get most of the water out of a canoe in the middle of the lake. Ben and Preston moved to one end of the canoe and pushed down with their combined weight and strength. The canoe practically leaped out of the lake, leaving a much smaller amount of water inside the boat.

Samuel and Jacob paddled over, carefully keeping the spare canoe between them and the boys in the water, so they wouldn't get caught again. They held it tight to allow all three boys to get back into their canoe, then pushed off and rounded up the paddles floating nearby. The canoe still held several inches of water, but it would make it to the dock with no problem. They headed back, cold and eager to dry off.

"I can't believe you guys let them do that to me." John frowned at his friends.

A white smile split Samuel's coffee-colored face. "Didn't want to get into the middle of this prank. Everybody would be out to get us if we blew the whistle."

"Yeah, I know." *The unwritten code.* They were obligated not to rat on the others, but as good friends, they stood guard to make sure he was in no danger. John understood, even if he didn't like it.

"Mr. Miles?"

A slender, black-haired man in a khaki uniform turned to face him. "Yes, John?" The twinkle in the Scoutmaster's eyes made him look like an overgrown boy, created to be a leader of boys. "What can I do for you?"

John didn't feel completely comfortable with his mission. "You know my grandmother is supposed to . . . to come talk to us on Friday night."

"Yes. Isn't she a distant relative of our founder, Lord Robert Baden-Powell?"

John shrugged. "That's what they say."

"We're honored to have her talk to us. That's particularly true this year. You know it's our 100th Anniversary." The BSA cap shaded the Scoutmaster's face from the blazing Texas sun.

John shoved his hands deep into the pockets of his gray, stone-washed shorts. The "Venturing" Boy Scout uniform shorts were comfortable as well as durable. "Yes, sir."

"So, what can I do for you?"

"Did you know she's writing a book on Lord Baden-Powell? It's supposed to be a history in connection with the anniversary. She really knows a lot about him, but even with all her research, she wants to get more of a handle on the man himself."

"I see." Mr. Miles's attention never wavered from John, even though a lot of noisy activities were going on around them.

"Do you?" John asked. "I'm not sure *I* do. She gave me an assignment. She wants me to talk to you and some of the other Scout leaders. She wants help in understanding what made Lord Baden-Powell do what he did. She feels sure the answer is right here . . . at this camp."

The Scoutmaster took off his cap, pulled a bandana from his hip pocket, and swiped the sweat from his brow. "And you'd rather do a book report or a theme paper than have to do this, right?"

"Yes sir, that's it." He sighed. "Not exactly how I planned to spend my week at camp."

"How will you get the information to her?"

"I don't know. She sent a video camera with me, but I don't know how to get any of it to her in time so she can use it in her speech."

Mr. Miles stared across the open field toward the trees in the distance, their limbs swaying in the slight breeze. "Well, Scouts aren't supposed to have computers or video games while they're here, but I could arrange for you to send your information to her by e-mail each night. That would give her time to work with it. The plan is for her to talk to the Scouts at the campfire Friday night, then at lunch the following day, when many of the parents will be here."

"Won't the file be too big to attach to an e-mail?"

The Scoutmaster's forehead wrinkled while he thought. "You're right. But I sometimes use an online site that allows you to upload large files. You send the link to the other person, who then downloads the file. We'll use that site."

What a load off my mind, John thought.

"Why don't we make her a little documentary?" Mr. Miles suggested. "We could send her all the information we have. In the process, a couple of you guys could earn a photography merit badge."

"Awesome!" John had always liked his Scoutmaster. His ideas sparked a lot of firsts in John's Scouting life.

"Let's start with a tour so your grandmother can see the layout of the camp. You can upload it to her tonight. By the time we're through, you may have the whole documentary." Mr. Miles crossed his arms and waited for John to latch on to the idea.

"Wow." Possibilities started churning in John's head. "Besides director, I'd need a cameraman and a sound man?"

"Yes, but to earn the merit badge, you'll have to alternate all three roles."

John smiled. "I have just the guys in mind."

"I thought you might."

The three of us'll make a good team.

————◆————

John and Mr. Miles opened the doors to the jeep and got out near the front, over-arching gate of the camp. Mr. Miles turned on the video camera and began to film John beside the main gate. "This is called an establishing shot," he said.

He sure knows a lot about many different things, John thought with pride. He knew he could learn a lot by watching his Scoutmaster set up the beginning of the video tour.

Mr. Miles shifted the camera away from the gate and began panning the gravel road that led downhill toward the campgrounds. The road weaved its way through the live oaks and shrubbery which kept tents, outbuildings, and other camp activities well hidden from the main highway.

Mr. Miles handed the video camera to John. "Your turn," he said with a smile.

John took the camera and tried out his best journalist voice. "I'm here at Camp M.K. Brown with Mr. Nathan Miles, my Scoutmaster. I take it this camp is named for someone, right?"

"It certainly is." Mr. Miles nodded, posing for the camera. "Brown was an oilman, a land speculator, and quite a public benefactor. He bought the land this camp sits on and gave it to the Scout Council, along with a substantial trust fund."

John gave a whistle. "Pretty cool."

"Hmm, would you call that a proper journalistic response?" Mr. Miles gave John a teasing frown.

John shook his head and tried again. "Why was Mr. Brown so interested in Scouting?"

"From what I understand, you could say he got in on the ground floor. You see, Mr. Brown was a good friend of Lord Baden-Powell. He was also a major influence in getting him to bring his Scouting program to the United States."

"Are you serious?" John almost lost his concentration. This was so interesting! He refocused. "How did Mr. Brown know him?"

Mr. Miles stared off into the distance. "Mr. Brown was born in England and served with the military in Africa. He met Lord Baden-Powell there, and they remained friends. He spent most of his life here in the states over in Pampa, Texas. That's about thirty miles east of here." He waved a hand in that direction. "He won a lot of honors and accolades in his life, but he was proud of saying he had received the coveted Silver Beaver award from the Adobe Walls Scout Council and is the only man to wear the designation of Chief Scout of the Council. That was before the Adobe Walls Council and the Llano Estacado Council merged to become the Golden Spread Council."

"Sounds like with all those honors, he really believed in it." John had never heard this story before, and it intrigued him. "What does M.K. stand for?"

Mr. Miles stared intently into the camera lens. "Montague Kingsmill Brown. He went by Monte before he took to calling himself M.K."

"What a mouthful. My grandmother is going to love this stuff." John noticed the quizzical look on his Scoutmaster's face and grinned. "The camera's off. That was me, not the journalist talking."

"Well, let's you and I give her a tour of the camp."

They climbed into the jeep and started out. Mr. Miles glanced at the camera in John's hand. "You'll need to decide how much you want to film me talking and how much you want to film the things on the tour that I'm pointing out. When you're doing that, you're both cameraman and director. Ready to start? Then say 'camera' and 'action.'"

This is really fun. John liked being in charge. He lifted the camera and pointed it out the window. "Ready? Camera. Action!"

The jeep crunched its way along the gravel road until Mr. Miles slowed down and pointed out a large half-circle of permanent, wooden benches in a small clearing. The benches looked a little like risers where they rested on a gentle slope surrounding a blackened area below.

"Coming up on your right is the council ring," Mr. Miles said. "This is where we have council fires, ceremonies, and such. It's where your grandmother will give her talk to the boys on Friday night. She'll stand next to the fire." The Scoutmaster indicated the ash-filled fire pit and then pointed out a tall, carved structure. "Behind the pit stands a twenty-foot-tall totem pole. I know a totem pole offends some people because they think it's an inappropriate religious symbol. Trust me. In Boy Scout circles, it's simply an Indian artifact and a decoration, nothing more."

John aimed the camera at the pole and panned it from the bottom to the top. "Looks like it's been here a long time."

Mr. Miles continued his travelogue. "The camp is very well-maintained, thanks to our grounds crew. We drive a whole herd of cows in a couple of times a year, and they graze the grass down. We have to clean up after them too, of course, but we put that to good use by mixing it with our compost pile."

During the last monologue, John panned the camera across an open field with tall grass. "So you might say that instead of paying a ground crew, the ground crew is paying for the pleasure of working here by providing compost!" John laughed at his own joke.

"You could say that."

They drove down the hill then up another one, which turned out to be the dam for the lake. It was a pretty little lake, with two docks. A small building held the aquatics gear; canoes and rowboats rested on racks nearby. John jumped out and started shooting video. He turned the camera on the Scoutmaster.

"The fishing is good." Mr. Miles pointed toward the body of water. "The lake is spring fed and stocked with crappie, catfish, bass, a ton of monster bluegills, and some channel cat. We practice 'catch and release,' except for boys who are going for their fishing merit badge. For that, you not only have to catch the fish, but you have to clean and cook them as well."

John climbed in, and the Scoutmaster drove the jeep up the hill to the archery range. Here, large, bright targets sat down-range on round bales of hay. They looked hard to miss, but John knew hitting one of those "bulls-eyes" was more difficult than it appeared. It took a lot of practice!

Next up was the rifle range. John pointed the camera at the custom anchor points for the shooters and the mound of dirt behind the targets to catch the bullets.

Turning back down the hill from the lake, they entered the camp area.

Mr. Miles continued. "That's the admin building on the hill. The staff camp area is on the right. The staff set their tents on concrete slabs, and there is an electrical outlet at each one. The building straight ahead is the dining hall. That bell in front came from the old Camp Kiowa over on the Canadian River. M. K. Brown did a lot for that camp too. Much of their stuff was moved over here when it closed. Get a good shot of that bell. It came off an old Santa Fe locomotive."

He waited while John got a close-up of the bell, then he resumed his narrative, pointing where John needed to aim the camera. "In front of the dining hall is the parade ground. The Scouts assemble there by troop each morning before breakfast for announcements and to post the colors. They do it again in the evening just before dinner. That's when we strike the colors."

"I know what post and strike means, but I don't think my grandmother does." John turned the camera to catch Mr. Miles's face.

"Put up and take down the flag."

They drove past the dining hall, made a circle of the campgrounds, and returned to their starting point near the parade ground. John filmed furiously to get it all on tape.

Mr. Miles brought the jeep to a stop and explained, "There are twelve primary campgrounds and a number of other areas we can use for campgrounds. Attendance at a week-long camp averages around 300 boys. To make it easier for your grandmother when she gets here, we made sure your troop is camped in this first site, next to the dining hall. She'll stay in the staff area just across the road. Over to the right, past the buildings, is a spring-fed creek that never runs dry."

The Scoutmaster put the jeep into gear and began to move off.

"Wait a second!" John exclaimed suddenly. A dark-gray creature with a narrow face and what looked like armor on its back rested next to the gravel road, just a short distance from the vehicle. "An armadillo!" he said. "I've never seen one this close-up—a live one, that is. Let's see if I can get a close-up shot of it."

"Good luck," Mr. Miles said with a grin.

Carefully, John began to open the door, but the armadillo took off, quickly lumbering into the brush. "Wow! I didn't know they were that fast."

"They run like rabbits," Mr. Miles said. "In fact, we call them rabbits on a half shell." He chuckled. "There's a lot of wildlife out here. We've got deer and rabbits and coyotes, even bobcats. And a grouchy old mountain lion wanders by now and then."

A shiver ran down John's spine. "That sounds dangerous."

"Nah. No mountain lion in his right mind is going to get near 300 hyperactive boys. Even if a lion happens to be hungry, it isn't suicidal." Mr. Miles stopped the jeep near the dining hall. "At this camp, boys can earn badges in plants, bugs, and all kinds of nature stuff. They can earn all of their outdoor-related badges here at camp." The Scoutmaster appeared finished with his tour.

John glanced over at him. "Is that it?"

"That's it. We'll send this to her later. Don't worry, son, this isn't going to be like a book report. We're going to help her out . . . and we're going to make it a lot of fun."

"It has been so far." John smiled to himself as he headed for his pitched tent.

CHAPTER TWO

THE BEGINNING OF SCOUTING

John walked through an area shaded by tall cottonwood, oak, locust, and elm trees. He proceeded into the Troop 80 campsite, taking a 360-degree shot. "This is our camp." The panorama shot took in the multi-colored pop-up tents, which surrounded a small clearing.

Each troop had a different campsite, with different equipment. The flaps on each tent in this camp were open, the inside made up neatly, and all gear squared away for inspection.

"Mother would love it if my room back home was this neat, wouldn't she? Well, maybe when I get back . . ." Even as John said the words, he knew he might be able to accomplish it for a little while, but eventually . . . well . . . a guy is a guy, after all.

He kept shooting as he walked. "This is my tent, and these are my tent-mates." The boys started hamming it up, mugging for the camera.

"Knock it off, guys. She's going to think you're a bunch of house apes."

They settled down and stared at the camera trained on them.

John turned off the camera. "Wait until you hear the deal I have for you."

He explained the documentary project and the chance for three of them to earn the photography merit badge. A couple of the boys already had strong merit-badge projects underway, but Samuel and Alex looked interested.

"I'd like to give it a try," Alex said.

"That's great!" John grinned at his friend's eagerness to join him on the project. Alex was a special and "differently-abled" Scout. Although Alex had special needs, his Down syndrome didn't seem to slow him down in the least. He enthusiastically participated in all aspects of Scouting life and was currently working toward his Eagle Badge. This photography project would fit him like a glove.

The rest of the boys thought John's idea sounded too much like schoolwork and went on to other activities.

"To start with, Scoutmaster Nathan Miles, Assistant Scoutmaster Jared Roberts, and Camp Director Noah Webster are sitting around in the leaders' tent. We need an interview from them that will set this all up. Samuel, you can be the cameraman, and we'll plug in this external microphone. Alex, you can handle the lighting and sound. Be sure to keep an eye on this sound meter so we're hearing everybody OK, and see that there's sufficient light at all times."

Alex nodded. "What are you gonna do?"

"Overall I'll be the director, but right now I'm the on-air personality. For us to get the badge, though, we'll have to alternate the jobs."

The three friends trooped over to the leaders' tent to start the interviews.

Mr. Roberts offered each of the boys a soda and took his seat. "Where should we start?"

They looked at John.

When John had everything set up the way he wanted it, he gave the command. "Everybody ready? Lights, camera, action." He paused. "We are in a special meeting at the leaders' tent, where research on Lord Baden-Powell will be shared to help the writer, Eleanor Clark, prepare her presentation on the subject." He introduced the men.

"Tell us what your grandmother said," Mr. Miles prompted John.

"She said she knows a lot about him, but it was all history and not very moving. I think she wants to know what made him tick, why he did the things he did. She wants to understand what it was in his background that made him want to start the Scouts."

"How about you, John? Does that interest you?"

He felt uncomfortable. "Well . . . I want to make my grandmother happy."

His Scoutmaster nodded and smiled. "That's a good start, but I hope we manage to get you interested, as well. He's one of your relatives, you know."

"Yes, I know. We believe he is."

The camp director pulled a bundle of notes from an oversized bag. "Do you have any of your research with you, Nathan?"

"As a matter of fact I do." Mr. Miles reached under his bunk and came up with a leather satchel. "I brought my notes on the chance that we really might get to compare notes with Mrs. Clark." He looked at the camera. "I guess in a way, we are."

"You've got a lot there. Where did you get your information?" John asked as Alex extended the microphone toward Mr. Miles.

"From family history and from books. I discovered some of this information at our local library; the rest I found online."

Mr. Webster, the camp director, glanced at each of the three Boy Scout video technicians. "Our illustrious camera crew is going to be a good test case. If we start to bore them too much, then the material is probably too boring to be included in the speech or the book."

"Isn't that right, John?" The Scoutmaster seemed intent on his answer.

"We know there's going to be a certain amount of history involved," John replied, "but what my grandmother wants to know is what history tells us about Lord Baden-Powell. That's my assignment."

"I've got a lot of miscellaneous facts." Mr. Miles held up a sheaf of papers. "But I haven't tried to draw any conclusions from them." He started sorting through his papers. "I know he became *Lord* Baden-Powell at the third World Jamboree, and it was the Prince of Wales himself who made the announcement."

Mr. Roberts glanced down at his papers. "Yes, I have that too."

"Listen." Mr. Miles looked up. "It's going to get pretty tiresome saying 'Lord Baden-Powell' all the time. Scouts have a whole list of acronyms they use for common words. The one for him is B-P. Or often they just call him 'Chief' for Chief Scout."

Noah Webster let out a breath. "That'll be a time saver."

Mr. Miles looked at another sheet. "Did you know he was a big-game hunter and loved to fish and play polo?"

Mr. Webster read from one of his sources. "Yes, but it wasn't *all* so-called manly stuff. He was a good water-color artist and a sculptor."

John shook his head. "I didn't know that. I guess there's a reason Scout merit badges cover so many areas. He did a lot of different things."

"Exactly, John," Mr. Webster agreed. "He was interested in a broad area of subjects."

Mr. Miles pulled out a different folder. "I knew B-P was a writer." He opened the folder and glanced at the information. "It says here he wrote thirty-two books, which helped pay for his Scouting travels. He didn't receive a salary for doing his Scouting activities, did you know? There's a whole list of honorary degrees, some twenty-eight Foreign Orders and decorations and such. There was no doubt the man was well-loved."

John cleared his throat. "Did you want me to tell you when I thought it was getting boring? Well, it is."

Mr. Miles glanced up. "It won't be boring to your grandmother. Did you know B-P returned to Africa—actually to Kenya—later in life, and that's where he died? He was eighty-three."

"No." John's head was beginning to ache from information overload. "I suppose it's good to know where a famous relative died and is buried."

Mr. Roberts frowned. "What's your assignment again?"

"To figure out why Lord Baden-Powell—B-P, that is—did what he did," John replied.

Mr. Miles pulled out another paper from his pile. "It says here that he's buried in a simple grave at Nyeri, within sight of Mount Kenya. On his headstone are these words: 'Robert Baden-Powell, Chief Scout of the World,' surrounded by the Boy Scout and Girl Guide badges."

"So?" John wondered what the big deal about that was.

"Don't you realize what that headstone means? It doesn't say 'Lord' Baden-Powell, nor does it say 'General.' In the final analysis, with all of the honors and the accolades he received over the years, it was Scouting—the boys and later the girls—that meant the most to him. That's what he was proud of."

"Oh." John brightened. He'd found the lead sentence for the essay. "I get it." He signaled Samuel to turn off the camera.

Looking around, he realized it was entirely too quiet. "Where's the rest of the troop?"

"They've gone to the archery range." A look of longing came over Samuel's face as he spoke.

John glanced toward the Scoutmaster.

Mr. Miles smiled and waved them on. "Go catch up."

A loud chorus of affirmations accompanied the three boys as they scurried down the path toward the archery range, pushing and shoving, each jockeying to be the first in line when they arrived.

John quickly outran the pack. "There's the range. I call first on that open target."

He glanced around to see where Philip, Ben, and Preston were. When each boy gave him a wide grin, he wondered what mischief they were planning as payback for pulling them into the water this morning.

CHAPTER THREE

THE ARCHERY RANGE

Samuel was once again filming, but this time John was in the spotlight. He notched the arrow, stiffened his arm, and pulled the string on the forty-pound bow to rest against his cheek. Then he sighted down the shaft of the arrow. He estimated the elevation needed for this range. He was aware that the three Scout leaders had wandered over to watch and were now sitting in the shade behind him. He also knew his grandmother would see him on the range. *C'mon, John, make your grandmother proud of you!*

He took a deep breath and held it, checked his aim one last time, and released the two fingers holding the string.

"*Owwww!*"

The bow dropped to his feet. His arm was red and scraped and stung like fire. So much for showing off his skills! His friends were preparing for their turns and looked up at the unearthly screech. Samuel looked over the camera and shook his head. "Dude, you got in too big a hurry, didn't you? Forgot your arm guard."

"Yeah." Alex stared at the target. "But look. It was a perfect shot."

They turned to look at the big, circular target and at the arrow protruding right from the middle.

Samuel turned the camera toward the target and zoomed in. "Sweet! Dead center."

"You think so?" Because of the pain, John hadn't even noticed.

"Look at it." Samuel turned the lens toward John.

John zeroed in on his arrow, and a giant smile split his face. He hadn't done such a bad job after all. He finished his turn on the range, then relinquished his place to the others waiting in line. He took his camera crew over to where the Scout leaders sat.

Time for me to be the cameraman. He videotaped them as they turned their attention back to their work. They traded notes, quickly deciding that the most efficient way to make use of time was to glance through each other's notes, looking for something they didn't have themselves.

"If you're trying to get a handle on B-P, the man"—Mr. Miles held up a handful of material—"the first thing you can't help but notice are the words 'God and country' over and over on every document, running through every thread of the material on Scouting. This was very important to him. It's clear he felt young men, actually *all* men for that matter, should be basing their lives on the bedrock of faith and patriotism."

"Yes." Mr. Roberts pushed his glasses farther up on his nose. "I have more material on the man himself, but you have a lot more on the history of Scouting. That attitude of faith and patriotism is just as clear in the material I have on his family, and on his military career."

24

Alex held the microphone close to his own mouth. "Are they always listed in that order—God and country?"

"Always." Mr. Miles scanned the document he held. "You'd expect a military man to place a high value on patriotism, but the two are always listed in this order: God and country. It's clear he felt the greatest attribute of a man or boy is his faith."

Mr. Roberts brushed back a blond lock of hair from his forehead. "A lot of people might find that surprising in a military man."

Mr. Webster cleared his throat, and Alex moved the microphone closer to him. "They shouldn't. Some of our greatest military leaders were men of great faith. Eisenhower, McArthur, Bradley, and even Patton, in spite of his filthy vocabulary. Others through the years are just as worthy of being named, but it seems like the men from our biggest war are the ones who come to mind."

Alex leaned closer to the papers in the camp director's lap. "I like the pictures. Are these Scouts? Their uniforms sure don't look like *our* uniforms."

Mr. Webster nodded. "Those uniforms look more like World War I doughboys than the way you picture Boy Scouts, don't they? The war hadn't started yet, but I guess that was how soldiers already dressed, and those were the uniforms they had available for Scouts."

Alex laughed. "They look like toy soldiers. I'm surprised they had uniforms that small." He put his finger on the top paper. "February 8, 1910. That's the date the Scouting program was chartered in the United States, isn't it?"

Mr. Miles held up one of his papers. "Yes, that's the official beginning of Scouting in this country, thus the date of the anniversary. But you shouldn't be surprised at seeing uniforms that fit. We often send young men not much older than you to fight our wars."

"Not much older than me?" Alex's eyes widened. "Off where people are shooting and dying?"

"That's right, and it's a shame. I suppose that's why B-P was used to working with boys that age."

Alex stepped back. "I can't imagine having to go off somewhere and fight in a war. I know I could never pass the physical, but still . . ."

"It's always been our youngest that fought our wars. Oh my, look at this." The camp director held up an old magazine. "When they purchased *Boys' Life* and made it the official Scout magazine, they hired Norman Rockwell as the art director. I really like his work."

"Yes, he had a knack for capturing the common man." Mr. Miles took the magazine and studied the cover. "Now I see why he portrayed boys in his artwork so often."

John had been taking quick glances at the line on the archery range while the leaders talked. "Hey, it's my turn on the range again."

"I'll take over the camera," Samuel said.

John handed him the camera before heading across the grassy field.

Samuel kept the camera on Mr. Roberts as he watched John go. "I'm afraid we're talking over his head."

"No." Mr. Miles watched John slip the arm guard on before picking up the bow. "He's plenty smart. But as to whether we're catching his interest, that's a different question." He looked at his stack of material. "Oh, look here. *Lessons from the Varsity of Life.* "

"It's an autobiography." Mr. Webster also held up a copy. "B-P wrote it in 1933."

"Which made him—"

"Seventy-six." The camp director finished the Scoutmaster's sentence.

"Could there be a better source than the man himself?" Mr. Roberts glanced from one man to the other.

Samuel tried to keep the camera on the man who was speaking, but it wasn't easy.

"Yes and no."

Samuel swiveled for a close-up of the Scoutmaster when he spoke. "B-P was a very modest man and had a strong tendency to downplay his accomplishments."

"I can see that," Mr. Roberts said. "The book opens with an apology about not wanting to seem egotistical. Ah . . ." The assistant Scoutmaster's face brightened. "You want to know what makes him tick? Here, in his own words, is something that will shed a little light on him. This is from *Varsity of Life*:

> "A thing that many young fellows don't seem to realize at first is that success depends on oneself and not on a kindly fate, nor on the interest of powerful friends. I have over and over again explained that the purpose of the Boy Scout and Girl Guide Movement is to build men and women as citizens endowed with the three H's namely, Health, Happiness and Helpfulness. The man or woman who succeeds in developing these three attributes has secured the main steps to success in this Life."

Alex smiled at the men, keeping the microphone steady. "That says a lot about him, doesn't it?"

"It says a barrelful." Mr. Roberts turned a few pages. "But there's another part further over in that same book that may be even more telling. Just a moment, let me find it. Here it is." He began to read:

> "Through the whole of my career in the Army there ran a vein—a fad or whatever you like to call it—that obsessed me and which, while adding zest to my work, came to be of use for the service. Later on it proved the connecting link between my two otherwise dissimilar lives. This was Scouting.
>
> "Scouting includes a rather wide range of work. Briefly, it is the art or science of gaining information. Before or during war, information about the enemy's preparations, his strength, his intentions, his country, his circumstances, his moves, etc., is vitally essential to a commander if he is to win success. The enemy, therefore, on his part, naturally keeps such details as secret as he can. Thus the job which falls to the fellow who has got to find these out is a difficult one and risky. If he does it in disguise he is called a spy, and is liable to be shot, while in uniform he is the more conspicuous as a Scout and equally liable to meet his end."

John returned from the range and whispered to Samuel. "What'd I miss?"

Samuel handed him the camera. "You can review the tape. Some of the reading is a little boring, but I think they're sorting out what your grandmother is looking for."

John turned the camera on the leaders just as Mr. Miles started talking. "If I'm not wrong, part of the so-called 'scouting' that he did while in the service was done out of uniform, right?"

"Yes," Mr. Webster answered, "which means that during part of his service, he was actually a spy for his government."

"What?" That caught John's full attention. "Are you saying Lord Baden-Powell was a *spy*?"

"For part of his career, yes." The camp director nodded toward the camera.

"A James Bond, 007, licensed-to-kill spy right in the family?" John was glad he came back when he did. What if he'd missed this?

"I doubt it was quite that flamboyant, but he certainly could have been put to death had he been caught." The intensity of the look on Mr. Webster's face emphasized the seriousness of his words.

"Man, there's more to this guy than I thought." John didn't want to miss another word.

Mr. Roberts cleared his throat. "There's a little more here I want to read:

> "To do effective work demands a good knowledge of military tactics and organizations. It demands also, to a very high degree, the qualities of personal initiative and imagination, as well as of the four Cs, which I have elsewhere

said go to make a soldier, namely, Courage, Commonsense, Cunning and Cheerful Co-operation. Consideration for self, for one's ease or one's safety doesn't come in. Scouting is certainly a fascinating game for the performer and worth all the risk, because of its immense value to his side."

He stopped reading and turned toward the camera. "You see, he actually talks about scouting being the thing that tied the two sides of his life together. The soldier, then in later years the Scout leader. But I'll admit it's hard for me to make the connection between scouting in the army and scouting as a suitable activity for boys."

All three men sat silently for a few minutes before Mr. Miles responded. "Boys, you have to be careful not to let the word 'scouting' get in the way of your understanding. Scouting is an activity, one that can be dangerous and deadly serious when done in wartime, or an activity to build young men and women when practiced by youth. Lord Baden-Powell understood how they were similar as well as how they differed. He understood how to use the same principles that allowed him to train effective soldiers and bring them to bear on the task of building young people."

At last John understood. "That makes more sense to me. I'm beginning to see."

Mr. Miles looked at his watch then pulled a paper from his pocket. "Aquatics. Specifically, swimming and canoeing. Boys, it's time to go to the lake."

The assistant Scoutmaster, Mr. Roberts, looked up. "I suggest we move our conference over there, where we can keep an eye on them."

John smiled to himself. *That's a good idea.*

——◆——

Samuel pulled his swimming trunks on, then rolled up his jeans and stuffed them in a bin next to those of the other boys. "I think we lost our leader . . . or leaders."

John glanced back over his shoulder. "They'll be along. They're talking about B-P. They've been studying him and really getting into this. I didn't say anything when we left because they had papers spread all over the table."

"It's kinda like those guys are helping your grandmother with her homework, isn't it?"

"I guess. Or helping me with mine. I'm the one she gave the assignment to. She knows so much about the guy that I'm surprised they'd know anything she didn't."

Samuel elbowed him in the ribs. "Well, you better quit worrying about that for now. You do know you have a 'gotcha' hanging over your head?"

For a moment, John stared at him. "What's a 'gotcha'?"

"You really turned the tables on Philip. He'll be looking to get even. You know, do something and then yell 'gotcha!' He won't rest until he gets you back."

"Yeah, I've been thinking about that too. I wish he'd get it over with. Then I could really forget about it."

CHAPTER FOUR

THE SNEAK ATTACK

John sat on the end of the dock, being as vigilant as humanly possible. It turned out that being watchful was only useful when your adversaries were *above* water, where you could see them.

He was still on the alert when a pair of cool, wet hands yanked him off the narrow dock and into the lake with a loud *splash*! He barely had time for a breath before he felt his swimming trunks being ripped away from his body. He thrashed and kicked, but it was no use. Whoever had attacked him was too quick.

John broke the surface of the water sputtering . . . and fighting mad.

But there was no one to fight.

His unseen adversary was gone, and with him, John's swimming trunks.

John scrabbled and treaded water, trying to figure out what to do. *I can't believe this.* No way could he walk back to camp *au natural,* so how would he get out of this mess? And he wasn't even sure who had done this to him.

His options were limited. He'd just ruled out the *au natural* option, so what was left? *I guess I could swim across the lake and hope there's nobody between me and the campsite there.* He knew the Troop 80 campsite was just down the creek, but he'd still have to get from the underbrush that lined the creek, across the parade ground, and back to the camp. Nope, that option wasn't in the cards, either. He was beginning to regret ever getting himself into this prank duel. Of course, it might be more that just a duel. Others could have joined in this time.

That only left one option, and he took it. Not far away on shore, relaxing in a folding chair along with the other leaders, sat his Scoutmaster. "Mr. Miles!" John shouted. Noise usually carried well over water, and John hoped he'd raised his voice loud enough to be heard. He needed his Scoutmaster's assistance, no doubt about it.

Mr. Miles rose from his chair. "Yes, John?" he called back.

"Could you . . . come out on the dock . . . for a minute?" John asked between breaths. He was a good swimmer, but treading water was beginning to wear him down.

Mr. Miles walked out onto the dock and squatted near the edge. "What do you need, John?"

"I have this small problem. Someone slipped up on me a while ago"—he took a deep breath and kept treading water—"pulled me into the lake, and jerked off my trunks while I was underwater."

He could tell that Mr. Miles was restraining a grin with difficulty. "I see. I suppose that would qualify as a problem, all right. How about if I leave a towel down by the end of the dock? You could wrap it around yourself and make it back to your tent with your dignity intact."

"That'd be great, Mr. Miles . . . thanks! I didn't know . . . what I was going to do."

"You aren't laboring under the impression that you're the first one this has ever happened to, are you?" The grin finally emerged before turning to a full-fledged smile.

"Maybe not, sir, but I bet . . . I bet I'm the first one at this camp it's ever happened to while his *grandmother* was watching the video." He shot a glance off to his far right, where Samuel was slowly panning the lake, the swimmers, and the canoes. He seemed to be having a grand time getting in some unrehearsed video shots.

The Scoutmaster followed John's gaze and pressed back another grin. "Okay, I'll give you that one. We can edit it before we send it off."

A few minutes later, with a towel wrapped tightly around his dripping body, John made his escape. As he disappeared inside his tent, he wondered why he hadn't heard a single laugh or "gotcha!"

———※◆※———

Nathan Miles returned to the row of folding chairs, where the other leaders sat.

Jared Roberts, the assistant Scoutmaster, shook his head. "The interplay between the boys never fails to amaze me."

Nathan grinned. "Friendships are made in Scouts that last a lifetime. And there are honored adversaries. You'll notice I didn't say enemies. These guys get into good-natured rivalry, troops compete against other troops, but at the end of the day, they're all still friends."

"It's a shame the whole world can't function like that, isn't it?"

Nathan dropped into the seat he had vacated when he went to John. "Would solve a lot of problems, wouldn't it?"

———

John had changed back into his uniform: yellow camp T-shirt, "Venturing" shorts, and well-worn tennis shoes. "You guys ready to go to the mess hall? They'll be serving soon."

"Are we filming that?" Samuel asked.

"You bet. Put the camera on me, and I'll do a lead-in." He cleared his throat and gestured for the camera to be turned on. "They've always called the dining room the mess hall. That's what they call it in the army too. We eat our noon meal here. Sometimes we may do breakfast or dinner in the camp if there's somebody who needs to work for their cooking merit badge, but even then most of the troop goes to the mess hall. Actually, the food is pretty good."

The camera panned to show the mess hall, an attractive building with sturdy tables in rows with small benches on either side. It was the only place in the camp where everyone could gather indoors.

Samuel zeroed in on John getting a metal tray with indentations in it to divide the food that was about to be unceremoniously dumped into it. He leaned over to whisper to the camera, "Our food generally ends up in sort of a big pile in the middle of the tray. I'll bet they handle yours very carefully when you get here."

As the boys slid their trays past the steam tables, smiling cafeteria workers put meat loaf, mashed potatoes, and gravy somewhere on the tray. A bored-looking Scout at the end added a piece of chocolate cake and a small carton of milk.

As quickly as they seated themselves at the table, the boys attacked their food. They paused when they discovered John was offering grace. The onslaught continued as soon as he said, "Amen." The boys sucked up the food like so many large vacuum cleaners.

A new boy, Daniel, leaned forward. "So what's on the agenda following the meal?"

"Over at that little log building we have Polaris."

Daniel gazed in the direction John was pointing. "What's 'Polaris'?"

"We divide up into patrols to go for a hike. We're given compass and map coordinates, and we have to use them to find the next point on our map. If we do it right, we find a stake with instructions to the following point—on and on—until we find our way back to camp. The patrol that does it the fastest is the winner."

Daniel wrinkled his forehead. "What prevents someone from just going out for a while and returning to camp ahead of everyone else?"

John was shocked. "We're Boy Scouts. We would *never* do that."

"Of course." Red crept up Daniel's cheeks.

"Besides, we have to bring in the notes from each of the checkpoints." John lowered his voice. "A confirmation of the contact, just to keep anyone from being tempted."

"The last time we went on this hike, John became a legend," Samuel said with a snicker. He was trying to eat and film at the same time, but it wasn't easy.

Daniel looked curious. "A legend?"

"Samuel!" John didn't try to hide his displeasure. "You aren't—"

"Of course I am."

"At least turn off the camera."

"Not a chance," Samuel said. "If her grandson is a legend, she should know about it."

John hid his face in his hands.

Samuel started narrating the story. "John was leading our patrol, and we were making good time. Up ahead he saw a snake in the path. Being a quick thinker, he scooped up a stick and threw it to scare the snake away."

"So he's a legend because he scared off a snake?" Daniel's tone told John that he didn't think that was anything special.

Ashton started laughing. "Not exactly. It turned out . . . it wasn't really . . . a snake in the path." He giggled between each phrase. "It was only a stick."

Daniel looked puzzled. "I don't understand why this is so funny."

John wished he didn't either. He also wished there was a hole for him to crawl into.

"It's funny because . . . it wasn't a stick he threw at it." Ashton dissolved into gales of laughter.

"You mean—?" Daniel put his hand over his mouth, trying to stifle a laugh.

"The only Boy Scout in the history of the camp"—Alex took over, because Ashton couldn't stop laughing—"who tried to scare a stick by throwing a snake at it."

Samuel got a solemn look on his face. "We've tried to find out if there was an Indian word for 'boy-who-throws-snakes-at-sticks,' but there isn't."

John knew they were his friends, but he was glad the retelling was over. He wondered what his grandmother would think about the story.

CHAPTER FIVE

FOLLOW THE COMPASS

I t was Alex's turn to film as the small patrols of boys fanned out in every direction. He also had the microphone. Just before he extended it to the Scoutmaster, he asked, "Why aren't there adult leaders with them on this hike?"

"That would defeat the purpose of who we are," Mr. Miles explained. "The older boys—patrol leaders—have been taught to accept responsibility, and the younger ones are learning to someday take their place. We aren't just providing a place for kids to come and have fun, we're molding young men, just as Lord Baden-Powell envisioned. However, there are adult observers keeping an eye on things."

The camp director, Noah Webster, sat in front of the tent, staring at the small white clouds that drifted overhead. "I gave this a lot of thought last night to see what else I might add to the process." He glanced over at Nathan Miles. "I work as a summer camp director because

41

it fits nicely with my 'day job' of being a middle-school principal. My summers are free." He grinned. "Everybody who looks at B-P focuses on his military record or his development of the Scouting organization. Perhaps I can give you a little insight into him from an educator's standpoint."

"I didn't know he had ever taught." Mr. Miles leaned forward with his forearms on his thighs.

"Perhaps not in a traditional classroom, but he taught, I can assure you," Mr. Webster said. "His concern for young people, their social lives, and their imaginations led him to develop what could be called an 'associational educational form.'"

Alex shook his head. "That doesn't mean anything to me."

"Let me put it another way," the camp director said with a smile. "B-P didn't do all that well in school. In fact, the classroom bored him much of the time. However, he came alive when he went out into the woods. The result was that he placed a high value on adventure, and on young people learning to work together and take responsibility. Instead of the lecture format that was so prominent back then, he favored a hands-on approach."

"I understand that." Alex tried hard not to move the camera. "I learn better by doing than I do by hearing."

"Exactly. When B-P published his *Scouting for Boys,* it was an immediate hit with educators and youth leaders. It even ended up being read and followed by a significant number of girls, who were attracted to the adventure as much as the boys were. The methods he employed in teaching core skills and values to young people significantly impacted the way our educational system changed and developed. However, it isn't something that's talked about much."

"An educational innovator." Mr. Miles sat up and leaned back in his chair. "Yet another side to him. He really was a complex man."

———※———

John's patrol included his friends Samuel, Ashton, and Jacob. They quickly followed their first two compass references and map coordinates to find the next two, and were now on the way to the third. Though hiking briskly, they were well aware of the old tortoise and the hare story. They had no intention of running all the way and running out of gas before they could finish. Many a tenderfoot had made that mistake.

"Are you guys going to help me tonight?" John didn't break stride.

"Help you do what?" Jacob glanced at him.

"I'm supposed to cook. That's all I have left to earn my First Class rank. I have to plan and prepare the meal, explaining all about the necessary utensils, preparation, cleanup, and the works to the merit-badge counselor. In this case, it'll be Mr. Greg White, who runs the dining hall. We're going to be filming it, so I really want to do a good job."

A couple of evenings during the camp, individual troops prepared their own meals, to give the boys a chance to earn badges necessary for advancement. At these times, instead of preparing meals in the dining hall, the cook came around to each of the campsites to approve what the boys were doing. He was the final judge for the awarding of the merit badge. He also judged the various meals and would present the "top hand" award in cooking. As Scouts learned and used skills, troops were constantly in competition with one another. Troop 80 had already taken the archery and rope-tying competition this week, but they had lost out on "best campsite" and aquatics.

Ashton grinned at John. "I've already passed that step. I used my grandfather's chili recipe and cooked up a big pan of cornbread to go with it. He helped me make a couple of pots of it before I came to camp, so I was ready. At most camps, they have a chili cook-off on Thursday night."

John hadn't thought of that. "I was planning to cook beef stew, but maybe I ought to do the chili contest instead. I want to do the cornbread either way. I've arranged for the ingredients from the mess hall, but I'll ask Mr. Miles if I can enter the contest instead. The troop has the Dutch ovens I need to cook in."

"Yes, I used those Dutch ovens with mine." Ashton nodded. "I'll be happy to help."

Samuel shook his head. "I don't mind helping, but I don't really know how to cook."

"That's the point of allowing helpers." John hoped he could convince all three friends to join him on the project. "You serve as helpers to learn what you need to know so you'll be ready to do it when your turn comes to earn that badge."

"I've already done that step too," Jacob said. "I roasted chicken over the fire on spits and cooked baked potatoes in the coals. I cooked a big pot of red beans to go with it and baked biscuits in a Dutch oven."

"Wow, that's pretty fancy." Ashton stared at him for a minute without missing a step on the trail. "Where'd you learn to do all that?"

"They used to have a Cowboy Campfire Cook-off in my town. To be in the pro division, you had to be a working ranch cook. I went out every year and learned everything I could."

"So you really *can* cook?" John couldn't believe his luck. Having someone who knew how to cook that well on his team would help them a lot.

"Yep, I can cook," Jacob said. "They had a guy there by the name of Richard Bolt. He was really good. I liked to hang out around his chuck wagon. He taught me how to make coffee with no bitterness and beans that wouldn't give you gas."

"Like all those cowboys in that old movie, *Blazing Saddles*?" Ashton asked.

"Exactly. He said a ranch cook had to make the best coffee, biscuits, and beans. What you learned after that was a bonus. He taught me to do a good job on all three." Jacob ducked his head as if he didn't really mean to brag.

He had John's full attention. "Maybe you could help me do biscuits instead of cornbread."

"If you want me to," Jacob replied with a frown, "but it can't be sourdough biscuits. I would've had to bring my sourdough starter to do that, and I didn't bring it."

"What is sourdough starter?" Samuel sounded more eager than he had earlier. "This cooking stuff is starting to interest me."

"Sourdough starter *is* really interesting," Jacob explained. "It's like having a pet. It's a batter of flour and water, but it has living yeast in it and bacteria. It's actually alive."

"Yuck." Samuel made a face.

"Mr. Bolt gave me a start from his own starter, and he got *his* start from his dad. It'll last almost forever, as long as you keep it fed. Think about it! When I make cowboy biscuits, a little bit of those biscuits might date back to when Mr. Bolt's dad was cooking for drovers on a trail drive. It's a living part of history."

"That is just too cool." John wished he could learn to cook something that had a history like that.

Jacob nodded. "I keep it in a glass container that has a rubber seal and a wire bail that holds it closed. It has to have a small hole in the top so it can breathe. I found the old jar in an antique store. I just make up some dough and use that starter instead of adding yeast. Makes great biscuits."

"How often do you have to feed it?" John wondered if his grandmother would like a start of sourdough.

"It's easier than having a dog. You don't have to feed it but once a week if you're keeping it in the fridge. You can't play with it like a dog though, and if you pet it you end up with sticky hands." Jacob laughed.

"Funny," Daniel said. He was a new boy and had been attached to their patrol. "But would you guys quit talking like a bunch of girls about cooking and hurry up? We're going to come in last."

"Chill out." John hurried up beside him. "Nobody ever beats us at map reading, and we've still got a lot to do today. We have to pace ourselves."

"And whoever told you that cooking is 'girl stuff' is nuts," Jacob added. "Most of the best chefs in the world are men, and believe me—they make big bucks."

"Okay, guys." John said. He stopped walking. "Here's our last checkpoint. Let's find the proof of contact, and we can double-time back to camp. We have to beat Troop 175."

CHAPTER SIX

THE MERIT BADGE

The ingredients for the meal were spread across the table. John checked each item off his list to make sure everything was there.

Jacob came up beside him. "It's like I told you. For cowboys, it's coffee, red beans, and sourdough bread. Anything else is trimmings and depends on what you have on hand to fix. Have you ever cooked over an open fire?"

"Nope." John grimaced. "What little cooking I've tried was in a kitchen and usually went in a microwave."

"Well, out here our primary tools are these Dutch—"

"Wait a second," John interrupted. "Let's make sure we get this videotaped for my grandmother. I'm sure she'd love to see this type of cooking." He looked around, saw Samuel approaching with the camera, and waved him over. "We need this on tape, Samuel."

Samuel hurried over, lifted the video camera to his eye, extended the microphone, and said, "OK. I'm ready. Now . . . action!"

Jacob began again. "Our primary tools for cooking over a fire are these Dutch ovens." He opened a couple of doors below the work board on the chuck box, which was mounted on their camp trailer.

Inside the cubbyhole, several of the cumbersome, heavy pots were nestled. They were made of cast iron and had big rims around the lids to hold hot coals.

Jacob took a hook and pulled one out by the handle. "To cook in one of these things, we rake hot coals away from the fire and set one of these big Dutch ovens on them."

Jacob had started a fire earlier, and now it burned merrily a few yards away. A good-sized bed of coals lay beneath the crackling flames. Jacob took a small shovel, scraped some coals away from the fire, and fashioned a nest out of the red-hot embers. Then he set the Dutch oven on them.

Samuel panned the fire, the coals, and the Dutch oven. "What's this pot for?" he asked for the benefit of John's grandmother.

"This Dutch oven is for the biscuits we've been mixing up."

The boys returned to the work board on the tailgate, where they quickly cut the dough into several large, white biscuits. They returned to the fire, biscuit dough in hand.

"We fill the inside of the Dutch oven with whatever we intend to cook," Jacob explained. He arranged the biscuits along the bottom of the pot and set the lid firmly in place. "Now we pile coals on top of the lid, which makes the biscuits cook evenly." He gave a long, contented sigh. "For some reason, food just tastes better prepared over a fire." He looked at John. "Got it?"

"Looks simple enough," John agreed. He'd been watching Jacob's every move. He didn't want to make a mistake.

"If you have any questions, you'd better ask me now, because once I get you oriented, you have to take over. You'll have to explain everything when the camp cook comes by to see what we're doing." Jacob put his hands on his hips and waited.

"No problem."

Alex wandered over. "Need some help, guys?"

"The first thing we need to do is chop up these onions." John pointed to a heap of them on the table.

"I handle a chopping knife like I have four hands." Alex held up his hands with his palms out. "I'll get started on them."

"All right, count your fingers before you begin, and try to end up with the same number of fingers when you're finished." Jacob smiled at him.

"Good idea," Alex agreed.

"Here." Jacob handed Ashton three iron rods and a chain. "Take these and make a small, three-legged teepee over the fire, then fasten them together with this short piece of chain. Just leave the end of the chain hanging down. And try not to burn yourself!"

"It's as good as done. I know what you need." Ashton hustled to get it done. Samuel followed with the ever-present video camera.

"The fire looks ready," John announced when the iron-rod teepee was finished.

"Thanks," Jacob said. "Take this *S* hook and hang this big stew pot on the chain you left hanging down over the fire." He handed the hook and a pot to John. "Now we need to fire the pot."

"Fire the pot?" Alex stopped chopping and glanced over at the boys by the fire.

"Fire the pot?" Samuel repeated. "What does that mean?" He gave John a look that told him he was asking the question for the benefit of the tape.

"It heats up the grease that has gone deep inside the metal," Jacob said. "Then we'll wipe it down good and rub on a fresh coat of cooking oil. That coating is what keeps the pot from rusting between the times it's used."

John appreciated his friends' help. He was glad a couple of them had already cooked outside like this.

Alex finished chopping up the onions and a couple of bell peppers. John put them in the pot with nothing but a little cooking oil.

"If you'll cook these down a bit," Jacob said, "we can put the chili meat in and brown it."

"Keep them stirred well," Ashton cautioned, "so they don't burn."

John worked on the pot for a few minutes. The delicious smell of the onions and peppers was making him hungry. "Dump that meat in here," he said. "I'll make sure it browns evenly."

When the ground beef landed on the vegetables, the pot sizzled and steam rose up. John really had to stir to keep the meat from lumping up too much.

"Okay." Jacob held out two spice tins. "Now dust the meat with this cumin and red pepper. Take this can of tomato paste and add it in to bind it all together. Stir it until the sauce starts coating the meat."

The boys watched closely. Samuel held the camera close to the action.

"Here's a spoon." Ashton handed it to John. "Try a bite of that meat and see if it tastes all right."

John blew on the bit of meat to cool it down then tasted it. "I'm no expert, but I think it needs salt."

The other boys tasted it and agreed. Alex passed the salt canister, and Jacob poured the sparkling white grains into his hand. "If you measure this little bit I poured out, you'll find it's very close to a teaspoonful. Mr. Bolt made me practice measuring different amounts of salt in my hand until I got it just right."

"I'm impressed," John said.

They sprinkled the salt over the meat, stirred it a while, then tasted it again.

"It tastes about right now." John grinned at his helpers.

"You're getting the hang of this," Jacob said. He clapped him on the shoulder. "I like to add diced tomatoes to my chili, and maybe a can of tomato sauce. Lots of people make it with no tomatoes or tomato sauce at all, but that's how I like it."

"Let's do it. I like a stronger tomato taste too." John added the sauce and stirred it in.

"You'll need to add a couple cans of water. Keep an eye on it as it cooks down. You'll need to add water to keep the consistency right."

Alex came over with another spice container. "This is the 'big gun' for making chili. Cayenne pepper. There are hotter peppers, but this'll do. You add a little at a time until you get the exact taste you want." He smacked his lips.

"I make mine on the mild side, then let people add more cayenne to suit individual tastes," Jacob said. "Lots of folks like beans in their chili too. But most chili cook-offs really look down on that. If we were going to use beans, we would have had to start them some time before we started the chili, to give them time to get soft."

"Okay, John." Ashton nodded toward the pot of chili. "While it's simmering, you need to check those biscuits so they don't burn, and think about getting the cornbread going."

The biscuits were browning nicely, so John pulled them away from the coals to keep them from burning. They would stay warm inside the oven until it was time to eat. He raked more coals to refresh the glowing nest of embers and settled another Dutch oven on top.

"This is a big pot," John said, returning to the chuck box, "and everybody's hungry. Maybe we ought to do two of these cornbread mixes." He held up a couple of pouches. "The directions are right on the back." He grinned.

"Yeah, you won't have a problem," Jacob agreed.

John measured the ingredients, mixed everything into a smooth batter, and hurried back to the fire.

"Now," Ashton said, "pour the batter into the pot so it spreads evenly over the bottom."

John followed Ashton's directions, while his friend continued to explain. "When you cook in a Dutch oven, you adjust the heat by adding hot coals to the lid or by taking them off. You're not just learning to cook biscuits, chili, and cornbread today; you're learning to cook in a Dutch oven. You only need to change the recipes a little, and you can cook a lot of things."

"Are you getting all this, Samuel?" John looked up at his friend.

"Yeah," Samuel replied, "but my mouth is watering so much it's hard to keep filming. I want to dig into this grub!"

By the time the judge came by, John had his chili sitting in the middle of the picnic table, along with the nicely browned cornbread and the hot, fluffy biscuits. He had spooned out a smaller portion of contest chili and worked it over with cayenne pepper, until it was sure to fry the throat of anybody who tasted it.

Mr. White, the camp cook, helped himself to a bowl of chili, a chunk of cornbread, and a biscuit. He walked around the cooking site and listened as John explained step by step how he had prepared the meal.

"What about cleanup?" Mr. White asked.

John was ready with his answers. "We took what was left after cleaning the onions out into the woods. Hopefully, something will eat it and not need to come into camp looking for food. As soon as the big pots are empty, we'll fill them with water and heat them up. We'll wash the dishes in the pots, then empty out the grey water, rinse the Dutch oven and the big stew pot well, then wipe them down with a fresh coat of cooking oil."

"You don't scour them?"

"No sir! The pots need that oil down deep in the metal to keep them from rusting. That's why we fire the pot before we use it. It brings out all the oil, and then we wipe it down before we put new oil in to cook. The fire disinfects everything."

"Good job, John. Your food is excellent. You seem to know what you're doing in a camp kitchen. I approve your application for your cooking merit badge."

"Thank you, sir." John wanted to thrust out his chest in pride, but he refrained. "And, Mr. White?"

"Yes?"

"I just want you to know that I have greatly underestimated what you do here at the camp. I can't imagine what's involved in cooking as many meals as you do for so many campers. I have a new respect for you, sir."

"Why thank you, John. I appreciate that."

———

After cleaning up, a number of the boys joined John and Jacob for a walk down by the creek. Samuel slapped John on the back. "Great grub, pal. I had no idea you could cook like that. You don't cook around the house, do you?"

"I just heat up something in the microwave," John admitted. "But I liked doing this. I may try cooking some more."

"Is that so?" Alex said with a smile.

"Jacob cooks quite a bit," John said. "He's studied at the elbow of a working ranch cook."

Jacob smiled, "Yes, his name was Richard Bolt. He was a really good cook."

"Get him to tell you about cowboy cooking," Samuel said. "He said he knows how to make cowboy coffee that isn't bitter, and red beans that don't give you gas."

"Oh, yeah." John had forgotten. "You never did tell us about that."

"Wait." Samuel grabbed the camera. "Let's add it to the video we took of the cooking. Your grandmother would like to hear this too, I bet."

Jacob ran a hand through his unruly mop of blonde hair as his blue eyes looked into the camera. "Mr. Bolt taught me. He said the key to making cowboy coffee is to put a couple of handfuls of coffee grounds into the big coffee pot, add water, then let it 'make' overnight in the wagon."

"*Cold* water?" John wondered how that would help.

"Yep, sort of like *sun tea*. The next morning you hang it high on the fire and heat it up good, but don't let it break into a boil. It's the boiling that gives coffee that little bit of bitterness. Boiling also brings the grounds up from the bottom of the pot."

John felt confused. "I've always been told that you throw egg shells in the coffee pot to settle the grounds."

"Yes, he told me that too, but he said if the coffee never breaks a boil, the grounds don't come up off the bottom, and then the egg shells aren't necessary."

"You don't say!" John wondered if his grandmother knew this.

"Makes really good-tasting coffee."

"You said something about beans with no gas?" John couldn't imagine how.

"I liked that one a lot. Mr. Bolt said most people never manage to pull it off because they're in too big of a hurry." Jacob grinned. "He said doing anything well takes time."

"So what does he do differently?" John pulled his ingredient list from his pocket, ready to write down what Jacob said.

"He showed me how to sort out the beans and take out any rocks or culls. Then you cover them with water and let them sit overnight to soften."

"Just like he does with the coffee?" John jotted that down.

Jacob nodded. "Just like the coffee. The next morning you put the pot of beans on a nest of coals and get them boiling."

"Huh?" John looked up from his notes. "It's bad for the coffee to boil but good for the beans?"

"Exactly. You do have to stir them a lot so they don't scorch. Even a few scorched beans in the pot will flavor the rest of them. Once you boil them a bit, you pour off the water, and whatever it is that causes gas pours out with the water."

"Who would've guessed?" John added that to his list.

"There's one more step," Jacob said. "When you fill the pot with fresh water, you toss in a couple of raw carrots. They absorb whatever is left that causes the gas. You don't boil the beans this time. You just let them simmer awhile until they're ready to eat. The longer they simmer, the richer that bean juice gets. And the more days you re-heat them, the better they get."

John kept writing.

Jacob grinned. "You know, John, when they cooked those beans on the trail, if a cowboy started giving the cook a hard time, he'd just slip that carrot into the cowboy's plate when he dished up the beans."

"Does that do what I think it does?" John grinned.

"It does. All the gas those other cowboys didn't get tends to be collected right there in that one carrot. And the cowboy doesn't know why he's having so much trouble. The old hands don't bother to say."

The boys standing around them burst out laughing.

John considered it for a minute. That might be a good prank to pull on someone at camp. He hoped Philip didn't get wind of it. John didn't think he'd like having it played on him.

CHAPTER SEVEN

SEARCHING FOR ANSWERS

John led the camera crew on a prowl of the campsite, look-ing for a more material. They met a boy on the trail.

"Hold up a minute, would you?" John said to the boy. He turned toward Samuel, who was the camera man right then. "She'll get a kick out of this. Turn on the camera."

"This is my friend, Seven Johnson." John spoke toward the camera. "Seven, this is being videotaped for my grand-mother, Eleanor Clark."

Seven gave a bit of an embarrassed wave at the camera.

John knew just how to lead in. "Seven, that's an unusual nickname."

A pained expression flitted across Seven's face. "It's not a nickname."

"Really?"

"There are thirteen kids in our family, and my Pa ain't got much imagination." Seven kicked at a clod of dirt with his toe.

"You mean he numbered you instead of naming you?"

"Yeah, my brother Six and I are twins. He's here at camp too." He pointed toward a campsite across the field from where they were taping.

"That's really something."

"We're numbered One through Twelve, and the last one is named Joe. Pa is not only short on imagination, but he's a mite superstitious too."

John laughed. "All boys?"

"All but two. Mama wouldn't hold with the girls being numbered. So they are April Two and May Nine."

"Those wouldn't happen to be . . . ?"

"Yep, the months they were born in. Mama ain't got much more imagination than Pa. She calls them April and May, and he calls them Two and Nine."

By this time, Samuel was having great difficulty restraining his laughter.

Seven stared at Samuel for a moment. "You don't have to try to hold it in. It's real funny. Everybody laughs. It ain't quite as funny if you're on the receiving end though." Once again he ducked his head.

"I'm sorry, but it could be worse." John wanted to keep Seven from feeling too bad. "There was a Texas governor by the name of Jim Hogg. He was supposed to have named his girls Ima and Ura."

Seven chuckled. "Wow, that'd be even worse."

"It was only half true. There never was a girl named Ura. That was just a legend, but there really was an Ima Hogg. She became quite an important person in the state. Everybody remembered who she was."

"I bet they did." Seven started walking, and Samuel kept up with him. "Well, I best be getting on," Seven said. "They're waitin' on me."

John, Samuel, and Alex stopped and watched him go on down the trail.

———◆———

Late that afternoon, John, Alex, Jacob, and Samuel took a walk at the edge of the woods.

John gathered them around. "Guys, let's go sit on this log for a minute. I've got something I need to talk about."

They all took a seat. While the others chatted among themselves about what they were going to do the rest of the summer after camp, John pondered what to say for several minutes before he found a way to start.

He raised his head and held up his hand. "It's my friend Ben."

"Yeah?" Samuel scooted closer to John. "What about Ben?"

"Well, you guys know Scouts have a big focus on God and country. And Ben, he says he doesn't think he believes there's a God."

"I see." Samuel didn't seem to have much to say about that.

"I mean, we have a lot of boys here of different faiths. Most of them believe there's a God, only sometimes they have different names for him. Some of the boys believe there's a God, but they don't believe in Jesus." John stopped for a moment and stared at the tree limbs high above them. The leaves waved slowly in the evening breeze. "I know what *I* believe, but I'm no preacher. I don't know what to say to him."

Jacob nodded. "I know what you mean. It's difficult to talk to others about your belief in God. You certainly aren't alone there. I know lots of adults who have strong beliefs but don't know how to talk about them." He stood and spread his arms. "Then too, in a place like this, I'm sure they're concerned about how much religion you can talk about to other boys, if they might be of different faiths."

"Yeah, I get that, and I'll ask Mr. Miles. But I believe the rule is that it's all right for me to tell him what I believe if he asks me a direct question." That thought made John feel better.

Alex leaned over to look around Samuel. "And has he?"

"Yes, and I told him we'd talk about it, but I sure want to do it right."

Jacob turned back toward the group but kept standing. "What he decides to believe or not believe is probably the most important decision he'll ever make. He'll be deciding where he'll spend eternity."

"That's what bothers me. That's an awful lot to ask of a kid like me." John stood and glanced at each of them in turn. "Can you guys help me?"

"Why don't we each try to give him a little encouragement?" After listening to everyone else, Samuel finally had an opinion. "Maybe that wouldn't be as heavy as coming all at once."

"That'd be great." John sighed in relief.

"Right now we'd better hurry back or we'll be late for the campfire, not to mention the stories and the singing . . . and the S'mores." Alex rubbed his stomach.

"We wouldn't want to do that." John laughed as the group started off.

John was glad they turned back when they did. The campfire pit was busy when they arrived.

Gathered around the fire, boys were toasting marshmallows and making S'mores. An older Scout plucked a battered guitar, and they sang campfire songs between bites. The boys' voices rose and echoed across the lake. They jostled for position at the fire and elbowed each other, faces glowing in the reflected firelight. Here and there, boys blew out flaming marshmallows, slapped them on the graham cracker, and slipped on a piece of chocolate before putting on the top cracker. All around the fire, boys had chocolate mustaches and beards.

John slipped over to sit beside Mr. Miles. He leaned toward the Scoutmaster. "One of my friends has asked me about the faith component of Scouting. I'm not sure how to answer him."

Mr. Miles faced him with a thoughtful expression on his face. "John, in Scout meetings we've talked about the fact that God and country are two of the most important principles in Scouting, and God is always named first. The twelfth Scout law is 'A Scout is reverent,' and I believe it was put last for emphasis. Did you know BSA has a legal position that a person who does not believe in God cannot be a Scout leader?"

Surprised, John shook his head. "I didn't know that."

"The Scout Oath represents the basic values of Scouting. It addresses the issue of duty to God before duty to country, others, and self. The Boy Scouts of America believes that the principles set forth in the Scout Oath and Law *are* central to the Boy Scouts' goals."

John stared at the flames leaping around the wood in the campfire. He was fascinated by his Scout leader's words. "All right, I know that's right out of the book, but I know there are a number of different religions involved even here at this camp."

"There are. Listen, you nailed it. What I quoted from the Scout Oath came right out of a legal paper they gave us for handling just this sort of thing." Mr. Miles pulled his marshmallow from the flames and blew on it.

"But I thought there were religious badges that could be earned."

"There are." He popped the charred, gooey mess into his mouth without adding the crackers and chocolate. "And even though BSA encourages young men to be reverent, this religious award program was developed by various religious groups to encourage youth to grow stronger in their faith. The programs—and you notice I'm saying it plural—are approved by BSA, and the badges can absolutely be worn on the uniform. However, each religious organization develops and administers its own religious program." He licked the sticky residue from his fingers then pulled a bandana from his back pocket to dry them.

"So, if a boy comes to you and wants some religious guidance . . . ?" John couldn't let this discussion end until he had the answers he needed.

"Most troops have a chaplain, and that's who would talk to him. This troop is sponsored by the Methodist Church. The pastor doubles as our chaplain, but he isn't here at camp right now." Mr. Miles leaned forward with his forearms on his thighs.

"And what if the boy is just starting to question the need to find faith? What if he doesn't belong to any religious organization?" John wanted to know.

"Then we're supposed to suggest he visit some churches, find something that seems to make sense to him, and search for more answers there." One of the logs settled into the ashes, sending sparks flying into the dark night, almost as if to give emphasis to the Scoutmaster's words.

"I think that's where my friend is. He's thought on it enough that he has questions he's looking to have answered." John whooshed out a deep breath. "You're quoting a lot of rules to me, but you aren't answering my question. Are you saying I shouldn't try to convert him to my own faith? It seems like it, but then in the same breath you tell me how important faith is in Scouting and how important the twelfth law is to the development of the boy being reverent. We're supposed to believe in God, but the way we might help a friend do that is not made clear."

Mr. Miles gave a wry smile. "It's all about court cases and lawsuits, where we simply can't have an appearance of trying to push one particular religion—*any* religion. But when a boy comes to a chaplain for counseling, the chaplain can answer specific questions and provide faith answers."

"I see. So . . . if the boy asks direct questions?" John kept pushing for answers.

"We are always encouraged to give honest answers to direct questions. On a boy-to-boy level, if he asks what you believe, just tell him."

"That's clear enough." *Finally. Just what I needed to hear.*

"May I ask what the nature is of the questions the boy posed?" Mr. Miles asked.

"He asked me what my own beliefs are."

"Then you're free to answer, and to continue to answer as long as the questions persist, and in the direction the questions lead."

John noticed that the other boys were quieting down for the story-telling, and he hadn't even had a S'more. But this conversation had been more important than any sweet treat.

CHAPTER EIGHT

PLAYING BY THE RULES

Boy Scouts, dark nights, and campfires meant stories . . . campfire tales. Assistant Scoutmaster Jared Roberts was warming up as they sat down.

"Tell us a ghost story," a boy's voice called from the edge of the darkness.

"Actually, I had something different in mind." Mr. Roberts was a writer. He always had a story ready at hand. "How about a western?"

"Oh yeah." Jacob crossed his arms with his unruly mop of blond curls almost blocking his eyes. "I like westerns."

"I call this one 'The Gunfight.'" Mr. Roberts's eyebrows elevated mischievously as he exaggerated the words, *The Gunfight.*

The boys grinned and elbowed each other.

Mr. Roberts pulled out his notebook and began to read the story:

"Black Jack Carlton was dangerous, no two ways about it.

"Even on the best of days this would be true, but today word had filtered to him that Sandy Conover had been making a play for his girl. Considering his reputation with the sidearm holstered on his hip, it hardly seemed likely, but certainly no disputing the facts.

"Black Jack pulled his hat low over his eyes and stepped out into the street. He needed to find out. He needed to set things right. In Jack's world, reputation was everything. A challenge left unheeded, a gauntlet left lying in the dust, and he'd become fair game for every fast kid looking to make a name for himself. Fear had always been Jack's only protection. Fear of a reputation duly earned and jealously protected."

"Yeah," somebody yelled, "if you ain't got a rep, you got nothing!"

Mr. Roberts went on:

"Black Jack looked both ways down the quiet, even peaceful, street. No danger hung in the air like a black, ominous cloud, but he felt as if there should have been.

"His spurs jingled like tiny wind chimes as he headed down the walk. His hand stayed close to the butt of his weapon. A fast draw was essential, but accuracy made the difference. The first man to fire would not always be the last man standing.

"Was she worth it—Miss Jane of the golden hair and sparkling blue eyes? Maybe. And maybe it wasn't even about her. Maybe it was just about the challenge, the challenge he could not let stand."

The boys nodded.

"You have to take a dare," Samuel called out.

Mr. Roberts leaned toward the group. "I'm not so sure about that." He read:

"Black Jack reached the cross street and looked both ways before he cautiously stepped out where he could be seen. He removed his hat and wiped his forehead with his red bandanna before he retied it around his neck. Where could Conover be? Hiding, probably. He didn't have a reputation as a back shooter, but who knew the true colors anybody would show when it got right down to it?

"He crossed the street, keeping careful vigil . . . then he spied him. The young cowpoke with the sandy hair that had given him his name stepped out on the walk and squared himself to face Black Jack.

"'A shootout.' Someone gave a loud whisper.

"'You looking for me?' A carefree grin shone on Sandy's face.

"Black Jack wasn't impressed by the bravado. He'd seen it many times before. Seems there was always a youngster waiting to call him out, to try and make their reputation on him.

"'You know who I am,' Conover said.
"'I heard.'"

The assistant Scoutmaster gave each character his own voice.

"'Why'd you do it, Sandy? You had to know I'd come.'
"'You think I'm scared of you?'
"'You should be.'
"Sandy toyed with the butt of his own weapon and said, 'I don't think you're that fast.'
"'One way to find out.'
"They began to walk toward one another, hands hovering over their weapons, eyes locked. Their steps were slow and sure. As the distance decreased, the likelihood of getting hit increased. One would soon lose his nerve and draw. Sandy's hand started to move.
"'Jackie!'
"Both froze.
"'Yeah, Mom?'
"'You get in the house this instant. When your father finds out you kids have been shooting slingshots at each other again, he'll tan your hide.'"

Mr. Roberts closed the notebook. "The end."
"Are you kidding me?" Jacob stared at him, stunned. "Kids? I thought . . ."
Samuel shook his head. "I bit on that one big time."
There was laughter all around.

Ben turned to the Scoutmaster. "How about if you tell one, Mr. Miles?"

"A ghost story," the boy from the back of the group said again.

"How about a true story?" Mr. Miles answered.

"Does it have ghosts in it?" The Scout was persistent, if nothing else.

"No, it's an animal story, and I think appropriate for the surroundings. It happened a couple of weeks ago when we were sitting out under the awning of our RV down at Roaring Springs, Texas. It's a nice little membership camping ranch where we like to go camping. My wife and I were both reading. A movement caught my wife's attention and she said, 'Look at that.'"

"A roadrunner was coming down the road near our campsite. He stopped to pose in the familiar heads up, tail up pose, then took off at great speed, head and tail going parallel to the ground to make him more aerodynamically efficient. He was magnificent."

Ben sported a huge grin. "I like roadrunners."

"Ah, but the roadrunner was only one player to the drama." Mr. Miles paused before continuing. "As he passed under the big cottonwood in front of us, a *whiz* like a bullet came from the sky and swooped down on the hapless bird. The roadrunner picked up so much ground speed during the attack that he briefly became airborne, then he assumed his breakneck ground speed. We laughed and sympathized with the roadrunner for the unprovoked mockingbird attack."

"It *was* kinda sneaky." Samuel's eyes sparked with mischief. "I've seen mockingbirds in the park swoop down to ambush squirrels, cats, and even people who get too close to their nesting tree."

"Yes, but things are sometimes not what they appear. I watched the roadrunner's progress. It appeared that he was up to nothing more sinister than going over to watch people play golf for a while. He would follow a pair of golfers for several holes, evaluating their technique from a short distance away. It seemed to interest him no end."

"A golfing roadrunner? Who woulda thought?" Ben laughed.

"Tiring of this, he retraced his steps. He headed back up the road at a casual pace, then lit the afterburner to go under the tree at high speed. This time, Mrs. Mockingbird joined in the air assault, swooping and diving."

Jacob grinned. "That bird is a glutton for punishment."

The Scoutmaster continued. "The intense attack raged to the end of the block, where even though the way was clear to continue the attack, the birds broke off and returned to their tree. There was some sort of invisible line. Once the roadrunner had crossed it, he was safe.

"It soon became clear to us what was going on. An hour or so later, the pageant was repeated. If the roadrunner came along, and no mockingbird was present, he'd hang around until one showed up. They were clearly enjoying this. It happened every hour or so. We were fascinated."

"They were playing?" John had never heard of birds playing.

"Yes. Sometimes the roadrunner would win, and the interceptor squadron would get nowhere close. On occasion, they would buzz him so tightly as to make him airborne. It went on at intervals for two days.

"But apparently, birds have feelings that can get hurt, just like humans. I walked over to the bathhouse next to the golf course. As I came out, the roadrunner came by on his return trip. He passed very close, and I spoke to him. But he had no time for me. His eyes were set on the tree, about half a city block away, assessing the situation, preparing for his run.

"I could see him steel himself, assuming his head-up pose as he stood on the bathhouse lawn. I remained very still, not wanting to interrupt his concentration. Then, from out of nowhere a mockingbird bullet zipped in, caught him completely unawares, delivered a sound peck on the head, then gained altitude. The roadrunner took off, not down the usual path, but into the brush.

"He didn't come back an hour later like he usually did, nor in two or three hours as had been his habit. Over the next couple of days we saw the roadrunner on the periphery of our camp, moving through the brush or the campground, stopping to peer at the tree but not going near it. His attitude was as clear as if he were speaking aloud. He was indignant. He was hurt—not physically, but emotionally. The mockingbird had broken faith, had failed to play by the rules.

"The mockingbirds would see him across the campsite and go over to play the game in a new location, but the roadrunner ducked away and refused to play. It was a sad thing to see—old friends no longer speaking.

"We didn't see the breach healed while we were there. I told this story because there's a great lesson here in keeping faith with your friends."

"Yeah," John snickered, "particularly if your friends happen to be roadrunners. It looks to me like they have really long memories."

The comment reminded John that he too had a long memory, and Philip and his cohorts still hadn't played their "gotcha" prank on him. For a while it had slipped his mind. He glanced around the circle until he saw the three deep in conversation. Were they talking about him? Plotting how they would catch him unawares?

Not if I can help it.

CHAPTER NINE

A SCOUT IS REVERENT

Alex stuck his head into the tent. "We're having break-fast at the camp instead of the mess hall. Samuel is cooking something up for his badge requirement."

John swung his legs over the side of his cot and tousled his hair. "What's he fixing?"

"I dunno."

The other boys rushed over to the bathhouse to clean up. John grabbed his shorts and hopped on one foot while he pushed the other one through. His foot hit an obstruction, and he fell back on his rear. *Ouch!* He tried one more time, but his foot wouldn't go through. He tried the other leg. *Same thing.* He heard someone giggle and glanced toward the front of the tent. Someone was peeking around the opening. *Philip.*

"Gotcha!" He hollered before he sprinted away.

Finally! Now John could quit worrying about the prank. He studied the leg openings of his shorts, but they wouldn't open. Philip had sewed them shut. John made quick work of cutting and pulling out the threads so he could dress. Then he high-tailed it to the bathhouse.

As they made it back to the fire, Samuel reached over to take a coffeepot off a nest of coals by the fire and poured each a steaming cup. "Sugar? Milk?"

John stirred a spoonful of sugar into his coffee, then took a sip of the hot beverage before he set it down and focused the camera on the boys at their tasks.

Ben had settled four pieces of bread in a flat, square, wire "cage" with long handles. He was toasting them slowly over the fire.

Samuel squatted at the edge of the fire, turning sizzling bacon in a cast-iron skillet. He mugged for the camera and pointed. "There's the main course. Scrambled eggs ala onion."

Nestled in the coals at the edge of the fire sat a number of scooped out onion halves. The insides held scrambled eggs and diced onion. The outer layer of the onion blackened as the eggs cooked.

"That onion taste is going to seep all through those eggs by the time they're done." He leaned over and stirred the onion pots with a small stick.

John's mouth watered at the smell, and his stomach growled. Soon they were seated and sampling the concoction. It tasted as good as it smelled. A little salsa on top to complete the entrée and they all made short work of the dish.

After breakfast and a trip to wash up, the camera crew set up in the shade of a big elm tree, watching a group of boys. A pudgy, balding man was showing them how to tie a variety of knots.

John held one up.

"That's a sheep shank," one of the younger Scouts quickly told him.

"Very nice." John inspected the short piece of rope. "And what is a sheep shank used for?"

"Don't you know what a sheep shank is for?" The boy sounded surprised.

"For the camera," Alex said. He peeked out from behind the camera. It was his turn to run the equipment today.

"Oh, I see. You use it to shorten a piece of rope or maybe to strengthen a section of rope that has been damaged." The boy sounded like he was imitating a Scoutmaster.

"Very good." John gave him a thumbs-up. He glanced around the young group. "Show us another one."

A lively, redheaded boy with a multitude of freckles jumped up. "How about a bowline?"

"Fine." John motioned him to continue.

The boy passed the rope around his body and held both ends in front of him, making a loop in one side. "All right, let's see. The snake comes out of the hole, goes around the tree, and goes back in the hole . . ."

His tongue poked out of his mouth a little as he concentrated on bringing the rope out of the loop he was holding and passing it around the length he held in his other hand. Then he passed it back through the loop and pulled it tight.

"There, that's a bowline."

"Good job." John high-fived him. "Do you know how the bowline is used?"

The boy nodded so vigorously that John was afraid he might hurt himself.

"Sailors use it to secure themselves if they're working on a deck in high seas. It can be used for a lot of other things too."

John thanked the two boys for their lessons on knots.

———◆———

After taking their daily tour through camp to find Boy Scout activities for the video, the boys returned the camera to the tent. John decided to go for a walk.

He found Ben by the lake, sitting on a log. His friend was absentmindedly flipping pebbles into the water.

John sat down on the log beside him and drew a deep breath before asking, "You ready to talk?"

Ben looked over at him with a hopeful expression and nodded. "I've been thinking on it. Every time we recite the Scout laws it says 'a Scout is reverent' but I'm not. I don't even know what that means, and it bothers me."

"Why does it bother you?" If John could figure out why it bothered him, maybe he would know exactly how to answer him.

"That's just it. I don't know. I just know that it's on my mind a lot lately."

John groaned. That wasn't much help. "I'm only supposed to answer questions, but I don't know how to do that if you don't know what it is you want to ask. Besides,

I don't know anything about other religions. I only know what I believe myself."

"All right, that's my question then." Ben jumped on that like a frog on a June bug. "What do you believe yourself?"

Since he'd been thinking about this for a while, John had a ready answer. "I believe in God and know that He cares about me. He helps me when I am in trouble or afraid."

"But how can you believe in something you can't feel or see?" Frustration shouted through Ben's tone. "How do I know He's really there? It seems to me that the more I find out, the more confused I get." He glanced toward John again. "I asked my Scout leader, and he suggested I visit churches of different faiths. He said I should use my common sense and see what did and didn't make sense to me, then delve in deeper once I started connecting with one." He heaved a sigh. "I'm not connecting."

"But you sure *seem* to want to connect."

With a huff, Ben continued. "Of course, I do. Everything in Scouts talks about God. I want to believe, but I just can't come up with anything that makes me believe He's really there."

John felt like he was treading water in a deep pool. "I know you're supposed to have that belief when you join up, but somebody telling you that you should believe a particular way is not a good way to acquire faith." *Where did those words come from?* Maybe God was helping him. "A belief in God is something you need to decide for yourself, not just borrow the faith of someone else."

"That's what I want to do," Ben said, "but how do I come to believe in something I can't see, hear, feel, or touch?"

When Ben kept returning to this question, John knew it was the heart of what they should talk about. "Well, lots of people don't like to read the Bible or go to church because they start thinking about things that can be uncomfortable."

"That's it exactly. I start questioning things in my life, and I get uncomfortable."

John stared at him a minute. "Do you think that maybe God is speaking to you?"

"Maybe. So what do I do?" The lines of confusion between Ben's eyes deepened.

"You need to spend time with someone who can show you how to find the answers you need in the Bible. Someone who won't tell you what to believe, but rather who can help you find the answers to the questions you have. That way you'll end up with something you believe yourself, not just something you grabbed onto because it sounds good."

"That's what I'm trying to do. It has to be somebody I trust and somebody I can understand." Ben took a deep breath. "I trust you, John."

A loud, brassy sound caught John's attention. "This is going to have to wait. They're blowing the bugle for assembly."

"Can we talk about it later?" Ben asked.

"Sure thing. I can't help but think there are people much more qualified to do this, but if it's me you trust, then I'm going to do what I can." *Okay, God, You're going to have to keep helping me.*

CHAPTER TEN

SADDLE UP

The Scouts hiked to a nearby ranch. Horseback riding was this morning's activity, a favorite with the boys. They sang marching songs as they walked down the road, one column on each side.

When they arrived at the ranch, they broke into a run. They rushed into the yard, eager to claim their mounts.

"Now, hold on there!" A strong voice roared over the clamor of running feet.

The boys slid to a stop, raising a cloud of dust.

Hank, the old ranch hand, came forward, walking on bowed legs. His well-worn jeans and plaid cowboy shirt testified to the fact that this was his life. He removed the stained cowboy hat from his head and wiped his forehead with a faded bandana. "That's no way to approach a horse."

With the boys trailing behind, Hank walked up to a row of horses tied to the rail fence and chose the nearest mount.

He lifted the stirrup and hung it over the saddle horn as he tightened the cinch. He pulled it tight and kept tension on it. Then he waited. When the horse exhaled, he tightened the cinch a bit more.

"These aren't working ranch mounts," Hank explained. "These guys are livery horses. They'll pooch their old stomachs out so they end up with a nice loose cinch if we let 'em. Sometimes I have to give 'em the knee to let 'em know I'm onto their little game and make 'em let out the air they're holding."

He gave the boys a firm look. "If these here were high-spirited ranch horses and you ran up on 'em that way, they might decide you was a critter of some kind and take it on themselves to kick you into the middle of next week."

After finishing with the cinch, Hank let the stirrup down and moved on down the line. "As it is, these 'hay-burners' tote tourists for a living. It's a pretty good life. They take a little trail ride two or three times a day, not much effort involved. In return, they're cared for and fed. Pretty easy life."

He finished tightening the cinches and turned. "Who's ridden before?"

Jacob and Alex held up their hands.

"Every chance I get," Jacob said.

"I ride all the time." A big smile spread across Alex's face.

The ranch hand nodded to Jacob. "Reckon you'll ride point. That'll be Sundowner. He's a retired racehorse."

Jacob walked around to the left side of the horse, put his left foot in the stirrup, and swung up on his mount in one easy motion.

"Yep, reckon you've ridden before." Hank looked at Alex. "You'll be on Ole Tony and riding drag, bringing up the rear, making sure everybody keeps up."

Alex nodded. "Can I get a little boost, guys?"

Having made that one small concession to get up on his horse, Alex looked very much at home in the saddle.

The ranch hand motioned to John. "I think I'll put you on Buttermilk."

After he got the boys mounted, he walked around, lengthening or shortening stirrups to suit the length of each leg and continued his dialogue. "You can't get lost. These guys know their job. What they want more than anything else is to get back to this barn and get you off their backs." He grinned. "You quit controlling 'em, and they'll come home, sure as shootin'. They aren't going to run, so there's no point in trying. They'll give you a spirited little trot if you do it right, but don't expect to run any races. All right, Mr. Trail Boss, lead 'em out of here."

Jacob led them down the road at a trot. Most of the boys rattled in the saddle like rocks in a bucket.

The ranch hand shouted, "Use those legs like shock absorbers, boys, or they'll beat you to death."

Jacob pulled on the reins, slowed to a walk, and turned off onto one of the riding trails. Whether the boys wanted to follow or not didn't matter. The horses pulled up and stayed in line.

⊷•⊶

Nathan Miles and Jared Roberts took seats in the tree-shaded ranch yard as Hank went to the barn to do chores.

They got their notes out and started looking through them.

Mr. Miles put the camera on a tripod. "I guess we're our own camera crew this morning."

"I have a wonderful account here written by Ellen K. Wade," Mr. Roberts said. He pulled out a sheet of paper from his stack. "She was B-P's secretary. It's titled 'The Piper of Pax: The Life Story of Sir Baden-Powell.' She talks about how his ideas for the Boy Scouts developed, piece by piece, while shaving or bathing or walking, often coming to her on small scraps of paper."

"I've read that. She called him 'The Chief,' short for Chief Scout. She was clearly quite devoted to him, and she married a guy who was a top Scout administrator."

"His name was Major Wade."

"That's it." Mr. Miles punctuated the remark by jabbing his finger in the air. "One thing I remember in Ellen Wade's writing was the comment that The Chief slept outdoors, winter and summer, on the balcony of Lady Baden-Powell's bedroom."

"Absolutely amazing."

The Scoutmaster nodded. "If there's anything that proves he loved the outdoors, that's it."

"I found that really interesting, but I keep coming back to this one B-P wrote himself, *The Varsity of Life*. He says in it that he kept being approached by people whose education had involved the use of his book *Aids to Scouting for Soldiers,* and he talked about spending time wondering if it was a calling he was supposed to pursue." Jared Roberts laid down the paper he'd been reading.

"I believe it was." Mr. Miles glanced toward where the boys had disappeared from view.

"As do I," Mr. Roberts agreed. "He clearly thought his life, his military service, all of it pointed him toward a calling of helping develop boys into men, and a little later it extended to girls. Listen to this."

Roberts began to read:

> "This is a point which is very often lost sight of. Those results showed estimable young men, able to read and write, well-behaved and amenable to discipline, and easily made into smart-looking parade soldiers-but without individuality or strength of character, utterly without resourcefulness, initiative or the guts for adventure.
>
> "Modern conditions of life with its artificiality were making them members of the herd with everything done for them and with the fetish of 'safety first' ever before their eyes."

Mr. Miles shook his head. "That was *one hundred* years ago."

Mr. Roberts nodded. "And what do we have today? A huge number of single moms raising kids. Not that I want to disparage the job they're doing, but there is no denying the lack of a strong male influence in the lives of these kids. Particularly for boys who lack a role model, this is a problem. One hundred years later, it has only gotten worse."

"So the calling B-P felt and the battle he joined is still raging."

"And we're on the front lines."

"Yes, we *are* on the front lines, and I believe providing the male bonding and that missing male influence and positive male role model is one of the most important functions of the Boy Scouts." Nathan's serious expression underlined his concern.

"Is that why the Scouts resisted becoming a co-ed organization so stringently?" The assistant Scoutmaster relaxed in his chair.

"That's exactly why. But it affects other things too." Mr. Miles leaned toward his companion, emphasizing his point. "When we Scouts go on a campout and my wife comes along, I am careful to point out that she is *no*t coming as a mother, but as a guest."

"I don't understand."

"The first time it happened, we got to the campsite and she got out and started doing stuff. I had to go get her, ask her to sit down, and hand her a cold drink. She looked perplexed. But she watched as the boys worked like a well-oiled machine laying out the camp, setting up tents, putting up the dining fly, starting a fire—step after step until the camp was in place. Then the boys designated to do so were well on their way to fixing our evening meal.

"My wife was amazed. She didn't know they could do it. Then she said, 'But why couldn't I help?' She still didn't get it. I told her she was either a guest or a mother. If she started mothering the boys, they would immediately allow her to do it, and she would have been setting up and cooking the meal. Boys surrender to mothering automatically. We do *not* want mothers on camping trips, but we are happy to have guests who will admire our camping skills and allow us to show off for them." Mr. Miles smiled.

"No mothers? That's interesting." Wrinkles still marred Mr. Roberts's brows.

"It's different with Cub Scouts. Those packs are run by mothers and just wouldn't be the same without them. I'm strictly talking about Boy Scouts."

"I see."

Mr. Miles smiled. "My wife found the transition very easy to make."

———•—•———

The boys continued to ride single file, down by the bubbling creek and up through a shady cottonwood grove.

"Not hard to imagine that we're back in the Old West, is it?" Jacob glanced back so Ben, who rode behind him, could hear. "I almost expect to look up and see some Kiowa braves riding down on us."

"I hope not." Ben grimaced as his horse stumbled. "These nags couldn't outrun my grandmother, and she uses a walker."

"You might be surprised what they could do with some fierce, painted warriors coming after them," Jacob suggested.

"I doubt it." Ben clung to the saddle horn as his horse turned and plodded up an incline.

"A friend of mine writes western books," Jacob said. "I love to listen to him tell stories or read his books."

John rode behind Ben. "Is that why you like western stuff so much, Jacob?" he asked.

"That's part of it. Did you know there was no such thing as a teenager before World War II?" It didn't matter whether

Jacob watched where he was going or not. The old ranch hand was right. The horses knew the way and followed each other.

"That's silly. Are you saying kids went from being twelve straight to being twenty?" John's horse started up the incline behind the other two.

"Nope, but the word 'teenager' didn't exist," Jacob replied. "My friend says that's because there wasn't a time that kids were given to grow up. They went straight from whatever school they were attending to working on the family farm or in the family store. That's why they used to have such big families. They needed the help." Jacob's saddle squeaked under him as he turned partway around so he could look at John and Ben.

John frowned. "You mean that if I'd lived back then I might already be working for a living?"

"There's no *might* to it. You would have been. Out in the Old West there were lots of cowboys who today would be considered teenagers. A bunch of the soldiers riding with the cavalry or going on trail drives back then wouldn't be old enough to vote today. Girls were married and having kids while still in their teens."

The horse stepped on a rock and gave a quick jump, almost unseating Jacob. He grabbed the saddle horn and steadied himself.

"I know Billy the Kid was pretty young," John said.

"Killed his first man at . . . like . . . fifteen or sixteen years of age," Jacob said. "He was supposed to have been about seventeen when he was in the Lincoln County wars. They were trying to catch him to hang him. Age didn't make a difference then. If you were old enough to kill a man, you were old enough to pay for it." He shuddered.

"You really know this stuff." John wished he knew as much about cowboys as Jacob did.

"I read a lot."

The sound of a horse's shrill whinny made everyone sit up in their saddles and take notice. Something had spooked Ben's horse, and he was suddenly off the trail, pitching and bucking. Ben held on for all he was worth.

The boys shouted encouragement. The horse pitched and crow-hopped several more times, then set his feet hard, sending Ben up and over the horse's head. He seemed to fly through the air forever, turning over slowly like an Olympic diver in the layout position. He finally landed on his rump, raising a cloud of dust. Then he turned to see where his horse was.

He needn't have bothered. The horse was gone before Ben hit the ground.

———◆———

Nathan Miles and Jared Roberts were still locked in discussion when the riderless horse trotted into the ranch yard and—as predicted—went straight to the barn. The two men hurried across the clearing to see Hank pull off the saddle and begin rubbing the animal down.

"What's the matter?" they asked in unison, alarm in their voices.

"One of the boys let his horse get away from him. I warned them what would happen if they did."

"But what if someone's hurt?" Mr. Miles wanted to head out to see.

"One of the boys that can ride will come and fetch help. And the whole mess of 'em know about first aid. I could go look for 'em, but they'd probably be home long before I found 'em."

"You can't track them?" Mr. Roberts frowned. "I thought all cowboys could track."

"Hard to track on a ranch where there are horses going all over the place every day."

"It doesn't seem right doing nothing." Nathan stared across the open land, hoping to catch a glimpse of at least one of the boys.

"Who says I'm doing nothing? I'm rubbing down this here horse and waiting until I know what I'm dealing with. This happens all the time, pal."

———

Ben sat on the hard ground with a dazed expression on his face. Jacob had taken out after the horse, but it had too much of a lead. As the ranch hand, Hank, had predicted, his horse was unwilling to go faster than a trot. He gave up and turned around. As he rode back to the group, several boys dismounted to see about Ben.

"Hold onto those reins or you'll be without horses too," Alex warned them.

Ben got up, a little wobbly on his feet.

"Are you all right?" Samuel asked, concern in his voice.

"I don't think anything got hurt but my pride." He rubbed his bottom. "Well, maybe that's not entirely true."

"You can ride with me." Jacob pointed behind his saddle.

Ben grimaced. "Right now the idea of sitting anywhere doesn't sound too appealing. I think I'll walk a bit."

"Well, we'd best head back. That horse is at the barn by now, and they'll be coming to check on us before long."

"Shouldn't we be doing first aid?" Alex frowned.

Ben smirked. "What kind of first aid do you do on a sore bottom? Put a tourniquet on it? I'll pass on that if you don't mind."

They maintained a leisurely pace while Ben limped alongside. After a while Ben looked up at Jacob. "You mind if I ask you something?"

"What's on your mind?"

"I've been talking to John about this business of believing in God."

"You don't believe in God?" Jacob sounded puzzled.

"I marked the application that I did when I joined, but actually. . ." Ben hesitated.

"I see. You want to know whether I believe it or not?"

"Do you?" Ben stared up at him, waiting for an answer.

"For a long time now. My family goes to church all the time. Listen, if it's something you're having trouble with, how about coming to church with me the Sunday after we get back? I'll take you in, and we'll sit down with our pastor. He's the chaplain for the troop too. He can help you sort it all out."

"You can't tell me?" Ben frowned

"I think I could, but this is way too important to mess up."

"I think I'll come with you. I need to get this stuff figured out."

"Great. When we get back to camp, I have a little New Testament you can have. You can do some reading between now and then. If you read the book of John, you'll come up with the questions you need to ask."

Mr. Miles looked relieved when the boys rode into the yard. Ben now had sore feet *and* a sore bottom. He elected to ride back to the campsite with the leaders in the Jeep rather than hike with the boys. He adopted a position of kneeling on the back seat and watching the boys hike by the side of the road.

"They'll do fine hiking back." Mr. Miles glanced at Ben in the rearview mirror. "We'll go on ahead and get you back to camp since that position looks uncomfortable. When we get there, you might want to consider putting your trunks on and spending a little time soaking in the lake."

Ben gave a hearty nod. "That sounds like a first-rate idea."

CHAPTER ELEVEN

DISASTER

When the hiking Scouts finally turned into the front gate at the camp, a boy ran to meet them. "Something terrible has happened!" They gathered around him.

"What is it?" John could tell the boy was upset.

"I think a bear attacked your camp. It's just awful."

The Scouts broke into a run for the campsite. From some distance away, they saw people lying everywhere. John's heart nearly stopped when he saw his Scoutmaster lying near his tent. "Oh, no!"

He ran straight to Mr. Miles. Relief set in as he saw the sign that read: *severe cut on arm and blow to head, unconscious from loss of blood.* He caught his breath and let it out slowly. "Disaster drill." Then John went into action. "If this was a real disaster, he'd be depending on me to take care of him."

First-aid kits came out all over camp. John cleaned the wounds, which smelled suspiciously like catsup, and put a dressing on the Scoutmaster's head. He placed a pressure dressing on the cut and used his neckerchief to fashion a sling for his arm.

"I've stabilized him for transport to the hospital," he announced.

The camp director had a broken leg. Samuel and Jacob were using tent poles to secure the leg so he could be transported. They used their neckerchiefs and short lengths of rope to completely immobilize the leg.

Assistant Scoutmaster Jared Roberts was labeled *dead*. A couple of boys put a blanket over him.

Alex didn't let it go at that. He got down and checked Mr. Roberts out. "Hey, I feel a faint pulse."

The Scouts were finishing up their individual treatments and ran over to where Alex knelt by the body.

Samuel picked up a nearby shaving mirror and held it to the man's mouth. "He's breathing."

"So, what's the first aid for 'supposed to be dead but breathing'? That isn't in the first aid manual." John stood above them.

"Sure it is," Samuel said. "There are no visible injuries, so there is nothing to treat. We just need to get him transported as quickly as possible and monitor him constantly to be ready to do CPR if he quits breathing again."

"There's just one little problem," Ben said.

Samuel stared up at him "What have we missed?"

"Who called 911? Who has the transport underway? We should have done that as soon as we saw what had happened."

"We couldn't *really* call 911." Alex stood up to face him. "Not on a drill."

"If we're simulating the activity, we should have simulated the call."

"Ben is right, guys." John came up behind them. "If this were the real thing, right now we'd be getting professional help on the way. It might be too late for Mr. Roberts, and Mr. Miles has probably gone into shock. He needs help much faster than it's going to get here. But I think the big lesson is that although we're administering first aid, we need to get them to professional medical help as soon as possible."

Mr. Miles sat up. "Good job, boys. You're exactly right. It's funny. The biggest test of the drill turned out to be the one we didn't even plan. Mr. Roberts was supposed to be dead, plain and simple. Discovering he still has a pulse took it to a whole new level. You're also right that even though you have done a good job of administering first aid, you should have sent someone for help right at the beginning."

The boys looked ashamed.

"I'm only coming down on this so you'll remember it in the future. The bottom line is that you did a fine job with your first aid. The bigger question is this: Could you have done as well if it had been for real?"

"I'd like to think so." Samuel crossed his arms.

John wanted to think so too.

—◆—

The boys headed back to the swimming area to practice their water safety skills. Mr. Miles and Mr. Roberts found spots in the shade along the lakeshore and settled down to watch. They had brought along a small table and set it up between them. Their notes about the life of Lord Baden-Powell were spread out on the tabletop.

Samuel stood nearby, camera in hand. If he wished he were in the water with the other boys, he didn't let on. He seemed to know this activity was an important addition to the video record.

"Can you tell me why everybody is jumping into the water in blue jeans instead of swimming trunks?" Samuel asked the two Scout leaders. He zoomed in on the figures in the lake.

"Great question," Nathan Miles replied. "It's an important water-safety skill. What do you do if you fall into deep water fully dressed? Watch. Each boy will swim into water over his head, pull his jeans off, and tie a knot in both legs," he explained. "Then he'll slap the jeans over his head and into the water to fill them with air."

As the Scoutmaster was speaking, John completed the maneuver. The air in his jeans made an acceptable flotation device. He floated comfortably and watched boy after boy complete the task. Soon all the boys were bobbing around, splashing water at each other.

The aquatics instructor blew his whistle. "All right, Scouts. Take your jeans to shore and hang them up to dry."

The boys clambered out of the water. The instructor then paired them off to practice water rescue, and they jumped back in the lake.

Samuel strolled onto the dock with the camera to get a closer view of the activities and to record the instructor's words. John waved and gave the camera his best grin. He hoped his grandmother was enjoying the video he and his friends were making. *If nothing else, she's really learning a lot about our camp life,* he thought.

"The preferred way to perform a water rescue is with a pole like this," the instructor said. He held up a long pole with a curve on one end. Using John as the swimmer "in trouble," he demonstrated how to use it to reach out and assist a person without putting the rescuer in danger.

Next he held up a round flotation device, to which a rope was attached. "Another good rescue method is this life ring."

Retaining a firm grip on the rope—so he could pull the boy in—he tossed the ring out to Jacob, who quickly latched on to the device. "Anything that floats can be used as rescue equipment," the instructor explained as he pulled Jacob toward the dock. "There may be a life vest lying around, maybe even a big, plastic jug or an air mattress."

Jacob released the ring, and the instructor hauled it out of the water. "But the bottom line is this: you may eventually have to go into the water after someone who is drowning. That is one of the most dangerous things you will ever do." His tone emphasized the seriousness. "A drowning person will panic and try to grab anything he can, even to the point where he's climbing all over the person trying to help him. The rescuer may find himself unable to stay above water, and the situation quickly turns into a double drowning."

Jacob held his hand up out of the water. "I swim pretty well, but I'm not sure I could do it with somebody hanging all over me."

"I thought we were supposed to knock them out," Ben piped up.

"You see that on TV a lot. Swim out a little farther, over your head, and tread water."

The instructor snatched up a life jacket, slipped into the water, and swam out to Ben.

Samuel zoomed in on the scene.

The instructor floated the life vest between Ben and himself. "OK, Ben. I want you to hit this vest as hard as you can."

Ben lifted his arm and smacked the vest several times. He shook his head. "I can't hit very hard with the drag of the water, especially while treading water at the same time. For sure I can't hit hard enough to knock somebody out."

"That's what I wanted you to see. I suppose someone has pulled it off, but mostly it's a dramatic invention on television. I wouldn't count on it to save my life. I might need to hit somebody to make them let go and to snap them out of their panic, but I'd never depend on it. However, while we're out here, it so happens that I'm in the perfect rescue position."

Ben laughed. "That's good, because I'm getting tired of treading water."

"Grab the life jacket."

Ben complied and let out a sigh of relief.

The instructor turned his head to the boys who were watching from the shallow water near shore. "The best way to attempt a water rescue is to take a flotation device like this and keep it between yourself and the victim. It doesn't look very heroic, but it is the safest way to do it."

John swam out to join Ben and the instructor. "What if you don't have anything you can use?" he asked.

"You just made a floatation device out of your pants. You can use a shirt. You can use a lot of things. The extra moments you spend getting something to help you can make the difference between a successful rescue or dying with the victim. Remember the four steps: *reach, row, throw, don't go.*"

The instructor blew out a deep breath. "All right. Now we're going to divide up and practice the worst-case scenario—a water rescue without a flotation device. We're talking last resort here. No one should *ever* attempt this type of rescue without advanced lifeguard training. These rescues have to be done from the back, and from the back only. Approaching a drowning person from the front is certain death for you both."

He glanced around at the dozen or so boys in the water. They appeared to be hanging on his every word. His gaze fell on Alex, who was treading water with the ease of a confident swimmer. "Come over here, Alex," he said.

With smooth, fast strokes, Alex made his way to the instructor. "Alex is an excellent swimmer. I hear he's won a number of first-place awards." He grinned at this "differently-abled" Scout, who looked pleased to be singled out as an example. "I want to use you to show the others how to rescue a swimmer in distress."

"Sure thing, sir," Alex replied with a smile.

The instructor showed the other boys how to approach a swimmer from the back, get his arm around the person's neck, and lay him out to tow him. "You see that Alex can't get his hands on me this way. If he tries to flip around and grab me, I push him away. You can't help your victims if they tie you up. Talk to them and try to calm them. Get them to see that the only way you can help them is if they cooperate. It would be terribly hard to have somebody drown right in front of you, but you'd still have a chance to get them to shore and resuscitate them that way. You have no chance at all if you allow them to drag you down with them. So remember, grab them from the back, and the back *only*."

The boys divided up, swam out to deep water, and began working on the technique.

Samuel filmed a few minutes more then turned off the camera and returned to where Mr. Miles and Mr. Roberts had been observing the activities from shore.

Mr. Roberts turned to Nathan Miles. "I'm glad the aquatics instructor emphasized how dangerous water rescue is. Most people think you can just jump in the water and save someone."

Mr. Miles was nodding. "I know. You see it on the news all the time—people drown trying to save somebody else. They think because they are good swimmers, they can do it. They don't realize that even the best swimmer can be taken down by a panicky person grabbing onto them."

The men looked up at Samuel. "I think you've caught some great footage of water safety instruction, Samuel," Mr. Miles said. "Why don't you leave the camera with us and join the boys. You have time to practice some skills yourself."

"Thanks, Mr. Miles," Samuel said with a grin. "I'd like that." He set the camera carefully on the make-shift table and headed for the lake.

CHAPTER TWELVE

5th WORLD JAMBOREE

The Scoutmaster and assistant Scoutmaster sat in the shade with their notes spread out as the boys continued their water-safety skills.

"Have we about exhausted our notes?" Mr. Miles held up a fistful of papers.

"Lord Baden-Powell was such a multifaceted man"— Mr. Roberts leaned back in his camp chair and rolled his shoulders—"I think we could study him for years and not run out of material."

Mr. Miles glanced at his helper and friend. "Let me put it this way then. Do you think we have enough to help Mrs. Clark prepare her talk and finish writing her book? I haven't heard back on the videos John has been uploading to her each night."

"I was talking to John at breakfast. She told him she was getting a better feel for B-P as a person. Before it was just a bunch of facts and family history." His gesture encompassed the boys in the lake. "Somehow seeing these boys in action makes B-P more real to her."

Mr. Miles blew out a relieved breath. "That's good to know. Well, let me turn on the camera. Have you seen this book B-P wrote, *Boy Scouts Beyond the Seas: My World Tour?*"

"I don't believe I have." Mr. Roberts leaned forward eagerly.

"This part should interest you. It was written in 1913. Scouting was still a fledgling operation here compared to England, and he talked about his visit to America. This ought to interest the boys, to see how it was back then." He read:

> "We had a fine rally of the Boy Scouts in New York. Some 4000 attended in a big drill-hall, and a smart lot they were.
>
> "They gave some very good displays which included bridge-building, first-aid, knot-tying with hawsers, wireless telegraphy, signaling, and drill.
>
> "There was rather more drill than we care about in England, and not such interesting displays of pioneer and life-saving work as we get here. But, no doubt, our American brothers will soon go on to these as they gain experience, because they are so much more interesting to the onlookers as well as being more amusing and instructive to the Scouts who carry them out.
>
> "The American boy is very like his British cousin to look at; that is, he is a bright, cheery, healthy-looking chap, but he is a little different

in some ways. For one thing I think he is sharper than the British boy and knows more for his age, and he has better chances of learning woodcraft than boys have at home.

"But at the same time, the Britisher, I think, sticks better to his work and carries out his duties a little more earnestly because he is expected to, and because it is his job.

"The best kind of British Scout does his work at a run, whereas the American is apt to do his in a more leisurely fashion, and on parade there is more talking and looking about in America than in England; but I think this is largely because the leaders of patrols in America have not yet taken charge of their Scouts quite so fully as they have done at home, and so this will come right in a very short time.

"At any rate, the American Scouts are jolly keen, sharp fellows, and, my word, they can cheer.

"The cordial way in which they received me was, indeed, astonishing and delightful. And when I told them that their brother Scouts in Great Britain would gladly welcome any of them in the Old Country, they sent up a cheer of greeting which might have been heard across the Atlantic."

Mr. Roberts smiled. "How awesome! I wonder if there is still a pronounced difference in Scouting between the two countries today, or between any countries for that matter."

"Different cultures do make a difference in the Scout program. I've seen that at the World Jamboree. But many things are the same, as well. The basics are the same no matter where the program exists."

Mr. Roberts pulled out more notes. "Speaking of the World Jamboree, last night I was looking at this publication on the 5th World Jamboree in the Netherlands in 1937."

"That was B-P's last Jamboree."

"Yes, and the last one before the War broke out. It says here they didn't have another World Jamboree for ten years. There's another piece here written by James E. West, the American Chief Scout Executive. He was describing the scene. I found it rather moving." Mr. Roberts began to read:

> "For a hundred minutes the grand parade went on, with cheers from the Scouts and from the audience, with bands playing, and with everyone present joining in the rollicking Jamboree song that was on the lips of every Dutch man and woman, from the tiniest tot to grandma herself.
>
> "The arena was again empty. But not for long. A roar, and twenty-six thousand Scouts stormed into the field in one surging mass of youth. It was an inspiring sight and a colorful one, of boys from all the world enthusiastically rallying around their leader and the Queen of the country they were visiting.
>
> "Another signal, and out of chaos came perfect order as everyone listened to the message of welcome from the Queen of the Netherlands. She told us how glad she was to

see us, reminded the Dutch Scouts in their own tongue of their obligations as hosts, and wished for the rest of us, in excellent English, that the days of the Jamboree would be marked by true Scout Spirit. As she finished by declaring the Jamboree opened, the solemn notes of the 'Wilhelmus,' the National Anthem of Holland, rang over the field, and everyone came to attention. Then another wave of cheers broke loose. Someone started the cry of 'B-P, B-P!' and in a moment the whole arena resounded with the chant.

"Lord Baden-Powell, the founder of Scouting and the Chief Scout of the World, lifted his hand, and we listened in silence while he expressed our thanks to the Queen for her presence and to the Dutch people for having undertaken this great Jamboree. More cheers followed his speech and still more cheers.

"The Jamboree was officially opened, there were days ahead of seeing the world, of making friends and of going in for that popular sport of all Jamborees: 'Change'—swapping and trading, whenever two boys met, the word 'change' was the key-word that started friendships between Scouts who possibly could not speak each others' language, but who nevertheless managed to get along famously."

Mr. Roberts slowly shook his head. "Wouldn't that have been something to see? I wish I had been there."

Mr. Miles nodded. "Yes, I'd have loved to have seen it as well."

Later that afternoon, John and Jacob found Ben sitting by the lake.

"We've been looking for you." John dropped on the ground beside his friend. "I told you we'd finish our talk. Jacob told me you and he have talked some, as well."

Jacob put his hand on Ben's shoulder. "Is it still bothering you?"

Ben looked up, a weak smile on his face. "More than ever."

Jacob sat down beside him too. "The Holy Spirit must be working on you."

"What does that mean?" Ben's face showed his confusion.

"In our church, we believe that when you start wrestling with this issue, the Holy Spirit begins to whisper to your heart."

John pulled his knees up and clasped his arms around his legs. "A lot of people say that their conscience is talking to them."

"I know all about my conscience working on me." Ben gave a rueful smile. "When I know I've done something I shouldn't have, it starts nagging me."

John smiled at Ben. "I'm with you on that. Is that what's going on now?"

"Yeah, only stronger than usual."

"That's because it's a really big question." Jacob picked up a rock and tossed it in the lake. He kept staring at the rings that spread out from the splash. "A question of whether you'll go to heaven or not. It's so important that neither of us feels qualified to help you with it."

"So, where are you on this?" John got serious. "How can we help?"

"I really want to believe in God . . ." Ben's voice trailed off on the breeze.

Jacob swiveled his head toward Ben. "So what's stopping you?"

"There's too much I don't understand." He paused for a long moment. "I don't want to be a sucker."

"I know exactly what you mean." John leaned back on his hands and pushed his legs toward the water. "We're all right there at some point. You hear people on both sides who are so sure of themselves. That's why they call it 'faith.' We reach a point where we just have to step out in faith and say we want to believe."

"He's right," Jacob agreed. "And when that happens, the same Holy Spirit who was causing you to feel so convicted goes to work helping you understand all the things a good Christian should know. You don't have to understand *everything* to get started. Young Christians never do. They just step out on faith. It'll all become clear very quickly, I promise."

"Look," John said, "Jacob and I go to the same church. You come to church with us when we get back, and we'll take you in and sit down with you and the pastor. All you have to do at this point is to say I *want* to believe there is a God. Our pastor will help you understand what to do in order to become a believer, and we'll be right there with you."

"People won't make fun of me?" A deep wrinkle creased Ben's brow.

"I wouldn't say that. Some people make fun of any religion, but if you're concerned about whether you're going to heaven or not, then you can't let people who are probably not making the trip themselves influence your decision. I can tell you that neither of us has ever lost a minute's sleep because somebody made fun of our faith."

"Then I'd be silly to let that hold me back." A hopeful note entered Ben's tone. "If you guys will go with me, I'd like to talk to your pastor."

"Either of us could probably tell you exactly what he's going to say, but I guess we both feel he'd do a better job. We'll come by and pick you up Sunday morning at nine, okay?" John clapped him on the shoulder.

"I appreciate it, guys," Ben said with a smile. "It's really been nagging at me, and I sure would like to put it to rest."

John stood up. "Glad to help, man." And he meant every word.

CHAPTER THIRTEEN

BE PREPARED

When John, Jacob, and Ben arrived at the campfire that night, the Scouts were singing. Right after they sat down, the song leader started playing the chords to "God Bless America." Voices young and old filled the night with strains of this beloved song.

"God bless America, land that I love . . ." John sang with gusto. This song was very close to every Scout's heart, and he enjoyed singing it.

Evidently this was the last song, because the song leader put his guitar up and glanced toward the assistant Scout leader.

Story time around the campfire was about to begin.

Mr. Roberts opened his notebook. "Before I get started, there's probably something I need to warn you about." He looked around at the faces, wide-eyed in the flickering light. "This one's a little spooky." Soft cries of "spooky?" rippled through the crowd of boys.

Mr. Roberts began to read his story:

> "I don't know which way you came when you arrived, but if you came in from the west you came through the town of Mobeetie, Texas. New Mobeetie is a small farming community, but old Mobeetie, well, it's the oldest town in the Texas Panhandle. It came into being because of Fort Elliott, and a former Texas Ranger captain by the name of 'Cap' Arrington became the sheriff. His jurisdiction covered the entire Texas Panhandle area.
>
> "If you go over there, the old jail is still standing, and you can see the gallows where they used to hang people convicted of various crimes. The problem is, not everybody who got hanged was guilty.
>
> "There was an old buffalo hunter by the name of Zeke Pardue. People today might say old Zeke was a bit eccentric. Eccentric is a nice way of saying he was different. Back then, they just called him 'crazy.'
>
> "Zeke kept to himself most of the time. An old man with white hair and a beard, he eked out a living by hunting his own food and occasionally working as a day laborer, when he found something he could turn his hand to. He was also inordinately fond of old John Barleycorn, which you would probably more readily recognize as whisky—drinking alcohol.
>
> "Zeke had a bad leg, crippled by a Comanche arrow. He dragged it behind him as he walked. You could hear Zeke coming with that distinctive walk: *drag . . . thump . . . drag . . . thump.*

112

The children made fun of him, laughing and mimicking his walk. Zeke paid them no mind.

"You could be around Zeke and not hear two words out of him if he wasn't asked a direct question. He didn't tolerate people well and only did so long enough to earn the necessary money to buy what supplies he needed and a few bottles to tide him over until the next time he went to town. Other than that, he went back to his small dugout a few miles out of town. He kept to himself.

"On one trip into town Zeke got into his bottle a little too heavy. The next morning, the sheriff found him passed out over by the corral. The problem was that a soldier by the name of Sam Hall was found dead a short distance away. Zeke was thrown into their new stone jail, was duly tried, and then strung up for murder. When they hanged him, they said his bad leg thrashed around, pointing first to this person and then to that person. One old woman pronounced it to be a bad sign."

Mr. Roberts looked around. The boys were listening, open mouthed, to the tale. Encouraged by the attention, he continued.

"You might think this sounds like the end of the story, but it was only the beginning. Everybody knows that when a man dies unjustly, his spirit can't rest, and that's what happened to old Zeke. His spirit just naturally wanted to clear his name.

113

"A prisoner in the jail started complaining that his cell would suddenly get very cold, and he'd wake up to see an old man with snow-white hair standing over him. He said the man asked him if he had killed Sam Hall. When the prisoner said 'no,' the old man would suddenly disappear. Apparently he wasn't satisfied with the answer, though, because the next thing he knew the old man was back, asking again.

"They didn't take him seriously, but a few days later the man was found dead in his cell. There wasn't a mark on him, and the doctor was unable to establish a cause of death.

"Sometime later a freighter drove his wagon into town. Over at the saloon, he tossed down several drinks, complaining about a crazy, old, white-headed man who flagged him down and asked for a ride. He said that after they had ridden for a bit, the old man asked him if he had killed Sam Hall. He told him no. The next thing the freighter knew, the old man was just plain gone. He didn't know where.

"'Strangest part of all,' the freighter said, 'his eyes looked like they were burning coals. Scariest thing I ever saw in my life.'

"The next morning the freighter unloaded his wagon and headed out. The wagon came back a couple of hours later with no driver. They backtracked and found him a few miles out of town . . . dead . . . not a mark on him."

The boys were murmuring softly to one another. Most seemed to be breathing a bit heavier. Mr. Roberts turned up the heat.

"A woman told her husband about an old man coming to her back door for a drink of water. When her husband didn't come in from the barn after dark, they found him dead in the barn, no apparent cause of death.

"Three suspicious deaths now had their attention. Sheriff Arrington investigated but didn't turn up any leads. Then a man came in to report vandalism out at the cemetery. Zeke's grave was open and the words 'I didn't do it' had been scrawled on the tombstone in blood.

"The sheriff decided that someone in sympathy with Zeke's cause was doing the killings to try and convince people that Zeke had been innocent, but he couldn't prove it and he couldn't catch the person. The most frequent comments about the spirit seemed to center around the old jail, as if that's where he hung out—no pun intended—until he felt the need to again try to clear his name.

"People talked about seeing an old man with fiery eyes, walking here and there: *drag . . . thump . . . drag . . . thump*, just a glimpse and then he was gone. It has come down from generation to generation. Every so often, another unexplained death occurs, and people know what it's all about.

"The town used to be much bigger than it is now. Another town sprang up nearby, the town of Wheeler. A lot of people took to living there, but it wasn't far enough away either. Only a couple hundred people live in Mobeetie now, and Old Mobeetie is a ghost town. And maybe that ghost's name is Zeke. But me, I don't believe in ghosts.

"One night, when I was on a campout right here at this camp, and the moon was full, I heard a noise. When I peeked out of my tent to take a look, I heard footsteps—strange ones—like somebody was dragging a leg: *drag . . . thump . . . drag . . . thump.* Then I saw an old man. He turned around, and I could see his face in the moonlight: pale and pasty. He looked sick, with flowing white hair and eyes like burning coals of fire.

"He seemed to be looking at me like he was making up his mind to ask me if I had killed Sam Hall. I suppose he decided I didn't look the type because he moved on, dragging that leg, then turned transparent and vanished.

"Like I said, I don't believe in ghosts. I'll tell you that flat out. But the stories persist, and the unexplained deaths continue. But not often. Just when the moon is full and the spirit is restless."

The boys' heads jerked up. A full moon shone bright in the summer sky. There were no sounds other than the occasional snap of the fire and the quick intake of a Scout's breath.

"And the problem is . . . that old jail is close . . . so very close."

"Hey!" Samuel suddenly leaped to his feet. "I hear something!"

The bright moonlight lit up the campsite like it was day, but back in the darkness of the trees came a sound.

Something was bumping through the brush. *Crash! Drag . . . thump . . . drag . . . thump. Crash! Drag . . . thump.*

"That sounds like somebody walking." John tried to keep his voice quiet. "And dragging a leg."

Suddenly, an eerie laugh erupted from the underbrush, and the boys disappeared faster than Mr. Roberts said the ghost had disappeared. In a heartbeat, they were burrowed deep in their bedrolls, clothes and all.

"You think we ought to remind them to brush their teeth?" Mr. Roberts asked.

Miles shook his head. "Not much chance of getting them out now."

Inside his tent, John was whispering. "You guys *do* know that was just one of the staff members making Mr. Roberts's story come to life."

"Sure." Ben's voice sounded a little wobbly. "I-I know th-that."

"Me too," the other two echoed.

"Anybody want to go check it out and see?" Ben controlled his voice this time.

"Not in *this* lifetime." John pulled the covers up over his head.

CHAPTER FOURTEEN

ON TARGET

Eleanor Clark arrived early the next morning.

The Scoutmaster greeted her at the front gate of the campgrounds. "I'm Nathan Miles, the Scoutmaster." A large smile spread across his handsome face. "The camp director took a boy who fell out of a tree to town. He thinks he may have broken his arm. He asked me to welcome you and get you settled."

Eleanor returned his warm smile. "Thank you."

"We're honored to have a relative of our founder come talk to us, particularly this year, our 100th Anniversary." He offered his hand.

Eleanor took his hand. He had a firm yet gentle grip. "I am delighted to be here and am looking forward to speaking to the boys," she said. "I have a great deal of knowledge about Lord Baden-Powell, yet I've had trouble really understanding the man. The videos you sent me this week have helped a lot. If it's all right, I would like to spend some time watching the boys and seeing the Scout program in action."

A growing excitement began to fill Eleanor's heart at the thought of being here—at the camp—watching the boys go about their Scouting activities. She really wanted to understand what had motivated Lord Baden-Powell to do all that he had done. She felt sure the answer rested among these boys, and among these dedicated Scout leaders. She was determined to discover it.

"Of course," Mr. Miles said, releasing her hand. "You are welcome to look around, observe, and talk to the boys and the leaders. Then, the plan is for you to talk to the Scouts during campfire tonight and again at lunch tomorrow, when a number of parents will be present."

"That's what I've been given to understand. I'm *really* looking forward to it."

Mr. Miles smiled. "I can't tell you how excited we are about not only your talk, but also about the book you're writing."

Eleanor returned his smile. "I've written a series of books for girls, but this new book about Lord Baden-Powell will be my first book aimed specifically at boys."

Mr. Miles nodded his approval. "And now, shall we settle you in?"

A few minutes later, they entered the campsite. Mr. Miles showed Eleanor to the tent where she would be staying. "I'll send for your grandson," he said, and left her to settle in.

Eleanor barely had time to unpack her things before John rushed in.

"Hi, Grand Doll!" A big smile split his tanned face. He threw his arms around her in a huge embrace.

Eleanor smiled when John called her "Grand Doll." It was the affectionate name all of her grandchildren called her. However, she suspected it would not be used in the presence of the other boys. *Too frilly*, she thought, *for a bunch of youngsters trying so hard to turn into young men.*

"I have so much to show you." His brown eyes sparkled. "This has already been a great week! I've gotten good at archery and at shooting a rifle, and I've been canoeing and swimming and hiking and—"

"Take a breath, John. Take a breath." Eleanor ran her hand through his unruly brown hair. "You don't have to tell me everything in one sentence."

"I'm really glad you're here, Grand Doll. All the boys know what you're here to talk about. They think it's pretty cool that I may be related to the man who founded Scouting." His pride caused his chest to expand.

"They'll be even more impressed when they find out more about him, but for now, how about that tour you promised me?"

John took his grandmother over to the Troop 80 campsite to meet his friends. He was proud of his Grand Doll. She was a stately lady with snow-white hair and an ever-present smile.

"You should have been here last night." Samuel seemed as excited as John to have Eleanor here. "The stories around the campfire were really good."

"Having a campfire without stories would be a gigantic waste of time," John said. "But the one last night kept me awake half the night."

"What kind of story kept you awake?" His grandmother sounded worried about him, and he liked the feeling.

"Aw, it was just an old ghost story." He hung his head so she wouldn't see him blush.

John's "Grand Doll" glanced around the campsite. "What's on your schedule for today?" she asked.

"You know we work for merit badges during most of our activities, don't you?" After she nodded, John continued. "I'm going to the rifle range this morning to work for my rifle-shooting merit badge. It's going to be fun."

Her eyebrows wrinkled together like they did when she worried about him. "Are you sure it's safe, John?"

He didn't want her to think it was dangerous. "Sure, it's safe. The instructors running the range are very good and watch out for our safety." He lifted an imaginary rifle into position. "We shoot from a position between a couple of posts set in the ground. There's no way we can point the rifle too far in either direction, even if we wanted to." While he explained, he moved the imaginary rifle a small distance in both directions. "We learn about handling guns and making sure they are unloaded at all times, except when we are actually getting ready to shoot targets. It's the supposedly unloaded gun that kills, you know?"

"I've always heard that." Grand Doll's frown melted away, but she didn't smile. "Even though Poppie had guns, they still make me nervous."

"It's better to know how to use them safely than to not know anything about them at all." John hoped his grand-mother would understand and not embarrass him around his friends.

"Yes, I suppose that makes sense." Finally, she smiled. "Well, let's go and I'll watch . . . from a safe distance, of course. Is your friend Alex as good at shooting as he is at archery? You bragged on the video about his skill with a bow and arrow."

John grinned. "He's even better with a rifle."

She thought about that for a moment. "Has Alex found it difficult to get all of you to accept him the way you do, with his special needs?"

"Not at all, Grand Doll! We pretty much treat him the same way we treat everybody else, and that's how he wants it. Alex is one special Boy Scout. He can handle most situations that come up, but we're there to give him a hand if he runs into trouble. One of his strengths is that he doesn't mind asking for a little help when he needs it—which isn't all that often. Besides"—John smiled wider—"you've seen on the video that he does a lot of things better than anyone else."

"I have indeed," Eleanor agreed with a nod. "The videos have opened my eyes to so many things about the Scouting experience. It was a wonderful idea to upload them to me each night. I don't feel quite the outsider I might have, if I hadn't been introduced to you and your friends—as well as to your Scout leaders—through the filming."

John went to the range, drew a .22 rifle, and began fitting the loop of the sling on his upper arm, adjusting it to give him a firm hold on the weapon.

As the range instructor worked getting the boys into position, Mr. Miles and Grand Doll sat in the shade.

"Are you ready for your talk tonight?" Mr. Miles asked.

Mrs. Clark nodded before answering. "I think I am. For both talks, actually. But I'm not through gathering information or trying to know B-P better. I've still got that book to write, you know. I can't tell you how much I enjoyed the videos and what a help they were in preparing. I believe the boys enjoyed doing them too."

"Oh, they had a ball." He smiled at how seriously the team had taken their assignment. They really earned their badges. "You would've thought they were shooting *Star Wars*."

Mr. Miles opened his folder, and Eleanor followed suit. She glanced through her notes.

The Scoutmaster shook his head. "Not sure what I can add at this point, but here's a reference we haven't talked about. This is the text from an interview with *The Listener Magazine* in 1937 where B-P downplays his role in starting the Scouting movement. He said, 'As a matter of fact I didn't actually start the Boy Scout movement, because the blooming thing started itself unseen. It started in 1908— but the microbe of Scouting had got me long before that. When I was a boy at Charterhouse I got a lot of fun out of trapping rabbits in woods that were out of bounds. If and when I caught one, which was not often, I skinned him and cooked him and ate him—and lived.'"

Eleanor folded her hands on top of the folder in her lap. "I think he was just being modest."

"Of course he was." Mr. Miles agreed. "But it is true when he wrote the book *Aid to Scouting*. It wasn't written for boys, but for soldiers. He wanted to train soldiers who were self-reliant and could fend for themselves without the support of the unit. It worked very well too. It was later on that he rewrote it for boys."

"As I understand it, that was after many schools and boys' organizations—even girls' organizations—were already using the version he had written for his soldiers."

"They were." The breeze ruffled the pages in his folder, so he closed it. "That's why he said Scouting started itself. It struck a chord in people and initially moved faster than if it had been formally organized. The organization of what was already blossoming came later. A lot of people and organizations helped get it off the ground, like the Boys' Brigade in England, E.T. Seaton's Woodcraft League, Daniel Beard's Sons of Daniel Boone and such, but there's no doubt that B-P's ideas provided the catalyst that brought them all together under the banner of the Boy Scouts."

John found his grandmother sitting outside her tent, reading. "Hi, Grand Doll."

She looked up with a smile. "Hello, John."

He plopped down in a camp chair next to her. "You ready for your talk?"

She chuckled. "Everybody keeps asking me that. Yes, I think I am."

"Are you scared?" He didn't mind talking to a small group of the boys he knew, but talking to a large group scared him spitless.

"Scared? No. I've given many speeches in my life." She leaned forward and looked him square in the eyes. "Am I a little nervous about it? I'd have to say yes to that. I've never talked to a group quite like this one, and I want to be sure I capture their interest."

Eleanor studied her grandson, recognizing the beginnings of the honorable man he would become intertwined with the small boy he used to be. "I want to make you proud of me, John."

"I'm already proud of you. Nothing could change that."

Eleanor laughed. "Sweet of you to say so, but I still want to do a good job for you."

"It's like the campfire tales, Grand Doll. We're used to them. Just tell us a story."

"Yes, I suppose that's right, isn't it?" She liked the sound of that. "Just another campfire story."

"You'll be great." John flashed his grandmother a smile. "We enjoyed gathering the information for you. Did we get enough for you to work with? Did we answer your big question about why B-P wanted to do all he did?"

"More than enough," Eleanor assured him. "After all, nobody knows all there is to know about anything. The more you study something, the more you find out there is a lot you still don't know." She thought about the videos she'd viewed during the week. "In spite of all we have studied this week, we've hardly touched on B-P's home and family life. And his military career would fill volumes all by itself. We've just been concentrating on the aspects of his life that we felt most impacted the founding of the Boy Scouts and—"

"And why he wanted to do it." John finished the sentence for her.

"That most of all. I could read what he did and how he did it. The 'why' of it all was harder to see."

"But you found the answer?"

Eleanor stared at the trees in the distance. "I believe I did." She turned to smile at John. "I think you boys showed it to me. You fulfilled your assignment to the letter."

"No way."

"Way." She loved it when she and her grandchildren could converse in the vernacular of the day.

"Wait till I tell the guys we helped you with your speech."

John jumped up and ran back toward his campsite, nearly bowling over the camp director as he rounded the corner of the tent.

Mr. Webster watched John run across the parade ground. "He seems to be on a rather important mission."

"He thinks he's bearing news that will improve his standing among the other boys," Eleanor explained.

"And will it?" He quirked an eyebrow.

Eleanor tried to stifle her smile. "That's not for me to say."

Mr. Webster removed his hat and wiped his forehead. "Well, are—?"

She silenced him with an upraised hand. "I *am* ready to give my talk."

He chuckled. "How'd you know I was going to ask that?"

"Lucky guess." She smiled.

"The boys are very excited about it."

"I surely hope I live up to their expectations."

"I have no doubt of it, Mrs. Clark. No doubt whatsoever."

CHAPTER FIFTEEN

THE ADVENTURER

Eleanor watched as a flaming arrow pierced the night like a miniature meteor, streaking across the clearing and embedding itself with a solid *thunk* into a log at the base of a carefully laid campfire. John had told her that the fire had been built strictly according to the Boy Scout manual, with kindling leading up to the small pieces that would catch, quickly leading up to the big logs that would provide the campfire for the evening.

As promised, the fire blazed quickly, lighting the faces of the Scouts who had been standing back for safety until the arrow had done its work. They moved forward to take their seats on the permanent benches that surrounded the fire in a semicircle. Eleanor knew this scene was repeated often during the summer, as Scouts came in to spend their week at camp. It had been this way year after year, generation after generation, but she sensed a special expectancy at this particular campfire.

Scoutmaster Miles walked into the circle of light. "Our speaker tonight is Mrs. Eleanor Clark. You all know this year is the 100th anniversary of the Boy Scouts. We invited her to come speak because the Chief Scout of the World was Lord Robert Baden-Powell. He and Mrs. Clark are distant relatives. Who better to tell his story, and what better occasion than the 100th anniversary? So pay close attention, because without the man she is going to tell you about, there would be no Boy Scouts."

John and Jacob brought a chair into the circle of light and set it down facing the boys, with its back to the fire. Eleanor took her seat and pulled out an index card. She held it up where she could read it by the light of the fire.

"Robert Stephenson Smyth Powell was born at 6 Stanhope Street (now 11 Stanhope Terrace) in London on February 22, 1857. He was the sixth son and the eighth of ten children of the Reverend Baden Powell, a professor at Oxford University. The names Robert and Stephenson were those of his godfather, the son of George Stephenson, the railway pioneer."

Eleanor put down the card and looked at the boys. She smiled. "Not all of it will be so boring, but I do want to give you some facts about him. I will drop those in now and again. But most of all, I want to tell you about the man.

"You see, when we start to wonder who Lord Baden-Powell was and why he would want to start an organization like the Scouts, we get the first clue from his own boyhood. His father died when he was only three. I believe that made him very aware of the need for a male influence in a young boy's life."

A few boys shifted in their seats, and the crackling of the fire played a welcome backdrop.

"The family was not well off, but young Robert received a scholarship to attend Charterhouse School in London. Fortunately for all of you, while he was there the school moved to Godalming, Surrey. Being away from the great city and in a rural setting changed things entirely for him."

Every boy had his attention trained on Mrs. Clark. None seemed to be bored by what she was relating.

"As a boy, he was always eager to learn new skills. He played music and—like the pranks I have observed since my arrival here—he also acted the clown at times. Most importantly, while a scholar at Charterhouse, he began to pursue his interest in the arts of scouting and woodcraft."

Eleanor glanced around at the faces lit by the campfire to the point where they seemed to be ablaze themselves. She had worried there would be too many facts, that the material would be too boring, too historical in nature to hold their interest, but so far, so good.

"As I said, I do not want this to be a plain, old, history lesson. If you have questions at any time, please put up your hand. I want this to—"

A hand shot up.

"Yes . . . Ashton, isn't it?" She hoped she remembered his name.

"Yes, ma'am. You said he was interested in scouting and woodcraft. How could that be? He was just a kid. It was a long time before he started the Scouts, wasn't it? So how could there have been such a thing as Scouting?"

"An excellent question, Ashton. The Boy Scouts had not begun at the time, but the function of scouting certainly existed. Armies throughout history used scouts to go out ahead of the main force and bring back reports of the terrain, or where the enemy might be lurking in ambush. Explorers, wagon trains, and cattle drives employed scouts to make sure the trail was free from danger. The scouts lived out in the open and depended on their wits and skills to stay alive. They reported back to the main group about the trail ahead: Indian sightings, safe places to ford rivers, or where the group could find an abundant supply of water. A scout sometimes meant the difference between life and death to a wagon train or the army."

"No kidding?" Ashton's hazel eyes changed from brown to green in the firelight, "I never thought about the Boy Scouts being a younger version of *that* kind of scout."

"Really?" Eleanor was glad the boys were connecting with what she said. "Camping, fire-building, archery, and canoeing. You never considered who might have needed those skills in days past?"

"Yeah." Jacob turned to look across at his friend. "Like John Wayne going out to scout for the cavalry."

Eleanor nodded. "Exactly."

Ashton shrugged. "I guess I should have known."

"B-P understood." Eleanor's gaze wandered over the boys, hoping to draw more of them into the discussion. "He 'stalked' his teachers in the woods surrounding the school, he caught, skinned, and cooked rabbits, and he learned to keep any telltale smoke from giving his position away. On holidays and weekends, he was always in search of adventure with his brothers. Once, they went on a yachting expedition around the south coast of England; another time they took a canoe trip all the way to the source of the Thames River."

"Our troop made our own canoes." Pride shone on John's face. "We take float trips in them."

"Are you beginning to see who paved the way for doing all of this?" Eleanor's lips turned up in a smile, thinking the boys were beginning to understand.

All around the circle, boys were nodding.

"B-P continued to use his school years to learn the skills he would use professionally, and would later use in founding the Boy Scout movement." She picked up the next card in her stack. "With these skills and interests, the next logical step was for B-P to take an open examination for the army. He took second place in the exam, allowing him to be commissioned straight into the 13th Hussars. He was even able to bypass the officer-training program, and as a result became their Honorary Colonel for thirty years."

A soft murmur made its way through the crowd. The boys were clearly impressed.

"B-P served his country in places like India, Afghanistan, and South Africa. He soon found himself, at the age of forty, in command of the 5th Dragoon Guards. In 1897, while serving with that command, he gave his first training in scouting and awarded soldiers who reached certain standards a badge based on the north point of the compass. Today's Scout Membership badge and the United States' adaptation are very similar."

Eleanor hadn't expected to have so much fun while talking to the boys. With each new statement, she watched a spark of understanding appear in more than one boy's eyes.

"B-P went on to become a Major General at the age of only forty-three," she continued. "Through his exploits, he became famous—and the hero of every boy—although he always minimized his own part and the value of his inspiring leadership. By using boys for responsible jobs during the siege of Mafeking, he learned the positive response youth gives to a challenge. During the 217-day siege, he wrote and published a book, *Aids to Scouting*, which reached a far wider readership than the military audience for whom it was intended. By the time B-P returned from his service, he found the book was being used by youth leaders and teachers all over the country. B-P set to work rewriting *Aids to Scouting*, this time for a younger readership. In 1907, he held an experimental camp on Brownsea Island in England to try out his ideas. He brought together twenty-two boys, some from public schools and some from working-class homes, and put them into camp under his leadership."

John shot up his hand but didn't wait to be recognized. "So that's when Scouting began?"

"Not officially." Eleanor gave him an indulgent smile. "But it was getting close to happening. *Scouting for Boys* was published in 1908, and sales of the book were tremendous. Boys formed themselves into Scout Patrols to try out B-P's ideas. What had been intended as a training aid for existing organizations became the handbook of a new and—ultimately—worldwide movement. Lord Baden-Powell's great understanding of boys obviously touched something fundamental in the youth of this country as well as other countries."

"The book, *Scouting for Boys*, has since been translated into many different languages and dialects," Scoutmaster Miles chimed in. "What happened when it came out was without fuss or ceremony and completely spontaneous. Boys began to form Scout troops all over the country. By September 1908, B-P had set up an office to deal with the large number of inquiries pouring in concerning the movement. You could say he had no choice but to make the organization a formal entity."

Eleanor nodded. "It spread like wildfire. Since he was only fifty-three, Lord Baden-Powell could have risen to the rank of Field Marshal, but King Edward VII suggested that he would do more valuable service for his country within the Boy Scout movement than anyone could hope to do as a soldier."

She leaned forward to be closer to her eager listeners.

"Now his enthusiasm and energy were directed to the development of Scouting. He traveled to all parts of the world, wherever he was most needed, to encourage their growth and give them the inspiration that he alone could give. He retired in 1910 to do just that, and the Boy Scouts of America was officially born.

"A fitting conclusion to my program tonight comes from the Chief himself. He wrote a message toward the end of his life. At the time he wrote it, he was still in comparatively good health, but he did want to capture a farewell message to his Scouts, for publication after his death."

She held up a piece of paper to the firelight and began to read:

"Dear Scouts,

"If you have ever seen the play *Peter Pan* you will remember how the pirate chief was always making his dying speech because he was afraid that possibly, when the time came for him to die, he might not have time to get it off his chest. It is much the same with me, and so, although I am not at this moment dying, I shall be doing so one of these days, and I want to send you a parting word of goodbye. Remember, it is the last time you will ever hear from me, so think it over.

"I have had a most happy life, and I want each one of you to have a happy life too. I believe that God put us in this jolly world to be happy and enjoy life. Happiness does not come from being rich, or merely being successful in your career, nor by self-indulgence. One step towards happiness is to make yourself healthy and strong while you are a boy, so that you can be useful and so you can enjoy life when you are a man.

"Nature study will show you how full of beautiful and wonderful things God has made the world for you to enjoy. Be contented with what you have got and make the best of it. Look on the bright side of things instead of the gloomy one.

"But the real way to get happiness is by giving out happiness to others. Try and leave this world a little better than you found it and when your turn comes to die, you can die happy in feeling that at any rate you have not wasted your time but have done your best. 'Be

Prepared!' This way, to live happy and to die happy—stick to your Scout Promise always, even after you have ceased to be a boy—and God help you to do it."

Eleanor folded the paper and tucked it away. The boys were silent. "At the first International Scout Jamboree in London in 1920, Lord Baden-Powell was unanimously acclaimed as 'Chief Scout of the World.' The greatest Scout of all time has sent you the message I just read. I hope you take it to heart. Thank you." She bowed her head slightly to indicate she was finished.

Scoutmaster Miles rose and gave the Scout sign. The Scouts all stood and mirrored his three-finger sign. "You have heard there's no such thing as an ex-marine. Neither is there such a thing as an ex-Scout. The values you learn, the imprint it makes upon your character if you fully get into the program will shape your life from now on. Presidents, astronauts, soldiers, and statesmen proudly list Scouting among their strongest accomplishments. Let's close out the campfire by reciting the Scout laws and the Scout oath."

"On my honor I will do my best, to do my duty to God and my country, to obey the Scout Law; to help other people at all times; to keep myself physically strong, mentally awake, and morally straight." The voices sounded more mature, if a bit shaky, as they spoke as one, holding the three-finger sign high.

The boys looked somber as Scoutmaster Miles asked, "What is the first Scout law?"

"A Scout is trustworthy," they repeated in unison.

"Yes, a Scout tells the truth. He keeps his promises. Honesty is part of his code of conduct. People can depend on him. And the second?"

"A Scout is loyal."

"A Scout is true to his family, Scout leaders, friends, school, and nation. Next."

"A Scout is helpful."

"A Scout is concerned about other people," Mr. Miles expanded. "He does things willingly for others without pay or reward. Next."

"A Scout is friendly."

"A Scout is a friend to all. He is a brother to other Scouts. He seeks to understand others. He respects those with ideas and customs other than his own. Next."

"A Scout is courteous."

"A Scout is polite to everyone regardless of age or position. He knows good manners make it easier for people to get along together. He shows respect."

They no longer needed prodding, "A Scout is kind."

"A Scout understands there is strength in being gentle," the Scoutmaster said. "He treats others as he wants to be treated. He does not hurt or kill harmless things without reason."

"A Scout is obedient."

"A Scout follows the rules of his family, school, and troop. He obeys the laws of his community and country. If he thinks these rules and laws are unfair, he tries to have them changed in an orderly manner rather than disobey them."

"A Scout is cheerful," the boys chimed.

"A Scout looks for the bright side of things. He cheerfully does tasks that come his way. He tries to make others happy."

Eleanor's eyes misted with tears as her gaze traveled over the young men so stalwart in their convictions.

"A Scout is thrifty."

"A Scout works to pay his way and to help others," Mr. Miles continued. "He saves for unforeseen needs. He protects and conserves natural resources. He carefully uses time and property."

"A Scout is brave."

"A Scout can face danger even if he is afraid. He has the courage to stand for what he thinks is right even if others laugh at or threaten him."

"A Scout is clean."

"A Scout keeps his body and mind fit and clean. He goes around with those who believe in living by these same ideals. He helps keep his home and community clean. And last but surely not least . . ."

"A Scout is reverent."

"A Scout is reverent toward God. He is faithful in his religious duties. He respects the beliefs of others. Now say them all together," Mr. Miles said.

"A Scout is trustworthy, loyal, helpful, friendly, courteous, kind, obedient, cheerful, thrifty, brave, clean, and reverent." The strong, young voices rang out across the clear Texas night.

Eleanor felt the conviction of these young men as an almost tangible force.

"Very good." Scoutmaster Miles turned the three-finger Scout sign into the corresponding three finger salute, which the Scouts returned. "Dismissed."

John ran up to his grandmother. "Grand Doll, that was great!" He took a closer look. "Are you crying?"

She brushed aside the dampness from her eyes. "Just tears of pride, John. Right now I'm feeling very proud of you and all these young men."

CHAPTER SIXTEEN

RESPECT AND HONOR

The boys looked sharp as they gathered for assembly the next morning. Today, instead of the more casual wear that had been the norm during the week, they had on their Scout uniforms. Lined up on the parade ground by troop, they came to attention and gave the Scout salute as the bugler played "To the Colors" and the flag was slowly hoisted up the pole. When it came to full staff, the two boys posting the colors stepped back and gave the salute as well.

The early morning rays cast a reddish glow on the camp, but high above the first direct light outlined the flag with a golden glow. Eleanor stood with her hand over her heart. The scene of all these young men showing such respect made her breath catch in her throat. A single tear rolled down her cheek.

The camp director moved up beside her. "I hope I never get to the point where that sight doesn't move me."

"Oh, I hope not, either." Eleanor brushed aside a tear.

The ceremony was concluded, and the boys went inside for breakfast.

"There has been a lot written about B-P, book after book," Mr. Webster said to Eleanor as he accompanied her toward the mess hall. "But I've never read or heard anything that tried to go beyond the history and seek to give us a glimpse of the man. I thought you did a fine job of getting into his skin."

"I hope so. That's why I came."

"Will you be giving it again for the parents?"

"No, I have something different in mind for them," Eleanor replied. "Maybe a few things will be repeated, but for the most part I have something I believe they need to hear."

"Well, that intrigues me. I look forward to it."

Eleanor smiled. *And so do I.*

—◆—

After breakfast Eleanor walked over to the Troop 80 campsite with John. The boys were busy striking camp, folding and putting up tents, getting ready to leave following the noon meal.

Nathan Miles stopped as he passed by. "If you would like, John can drive back with you tomorrow."

She smiled at her grandson. "I'd like that very much."

John ran over to help his tent mates strike their tent and pack the gear.

"I'm sorry I can't visit right now," the Scoutmaster apologized, "but this is rather a busy time for me until we get this done." He glanced toward the busy boys, then back

142

at Eleanor. "Would you like a cup of tea while you wait? Or there's coffee made."

"Tea would be fine. You go take care of business. I can fend for myself."

She settled into a camp chair and sipped the herb tea as she watched the camp come down quickly and efficiently. Every boy seemed to know his job and went about doing it with little coaching from anyone. Soon the gear was stashed in the trailer or on the bus, except for John's personal items, which sat where his tent used to be.

Samuel and Jacob came over to John.

"We'll help you carry your gear over to your grandmother's tent." Samuel lifted up some of the gear.

Eleanor stood and walked out of the camp with the boys. "What did you think of my talk last night? I can always use a little feedback."

All three boys immediately agreed they liked it.

"You didn't find it too boring?" She watched their faces to see if they were only being polite.

"Not a bit." Jacob's eyes flashed. "Sure, you threw in some stuff about where he was born and where he went to school and all that, but you made an interesting story out of it too."

"I feel like I got to know Lord Baden-Powell a little better." Samuel sounded like he had really thought about it. "I've heard about him before, of course, but to me he was always just this old man with a flat-brimmed hat. In every picture I've seen of him, he always has his arms folded. What's up with that?"

Eleanor laughed. "I never thought of that. I'm not going to wonder what his body language might suggest."

"I think it means he had his mind made up about something," Samuel suggested. "From what you were telling us, I'll bet he had his mind made up about a *lot* of things. He sounds like a man who knew what he thought and knew what he wanted."

"That's a good observation, Samuel. You may very well be right. How about you, John?"

"It was great. I'm really proud of you. All the guys I've talked to seem to feel just like these two. You were a big hit."

Eleanor studied the three boys. "I'm very pleased to hear that. I know you recognized material in the speech and know what a huge contribution you made gathering material for me."

The grins that spread across their faces told her all she needed to know.

The dining room was filled to overflowing, parents sitting with their sons all over the room. Chairs had been brought in, and a lot of those who didn't have family there sat around the edges of the room. Quite an assembly. Many would leave with their families after the meeting. Others would go back with their troop later that afternoon or on Sunday morning after chapel call.

The noise level in the room was a dull roar, with several hundred boys talking at once. A troop leader stepped to the front and raised his hand in the Scout sign.

"Signs up!" He barked.

Quickly the hands began to go up, giving the Scout sign. The noise level dropped as the hands went up, until the crowd settled down into silence. The camp director walked to the podium and smiled.

Eleanor looked out over the crowd. This had a different feel to it. The talk last night to the boys had been more like one of the campfire storytelling sessions. Easy and relaxed. This felt more like giving a speech.

"It's my pleasure this morning to introduce an award-winning author, Eleanor Clark," Mr. Miles said. "Mrs. Clark is a relative of Lord Baden-Powell, the founder of Scouting. It is most appropriate here in the year of the Boy Scouts of America's 100th anniversary for her to be talking to us."

Eleanor made her way to the podium. She smiled as she surveyed the crowd for what seemed like a long time before she began. Actually, it was but a matter of seconds. "Thank you, Scoutmaster Miles, Scout leaders, parents, and most of all, you boys. What a wonderful gathering: young men looking so smart in their uniforms; all these families listening to them babble like magpies as they tell about their experiences this week. I have been here only a couple of days, and I fear I shall have to guard my tongue or I may begin to babble about it myself.

"I have already taken the tour the boys gave you this afternoon. I saw the pride on the faces of you mothers when you saw the tents arranged in such military precision. I know you hold out great hope for those bedrooms back home."

A ripple of laughter went through the room as parents and sons exchanged glances. "I am not sure how transferable that particular skill will be to civilian life, however.

145

"I have been an observer the past couple of days, and I have seen the boys learn so much. At times it was almost as if I were watching them grow into young men right before my eyes. But as much as these boys have learned this past week, I feel it is I who has learned the most." She paused as the memories rushed over her. "I visited this camp to tell these Scouts exactly who the founder of this fine organization was, but in the end they showed *me* who he was." A murmur of admiration rose from the crowd as they took in this news.

"Lord Robert Baden-Powell was the founder of Scouting, and as Mr. Miles said, I am here because I believe he was a relative of mine. I had in my possession an amazing amount of information I intended to share with the boys."

She indicated the Scoutmaster with a wave of her hand. "I met Scoutmaster Miles and learned that he is a fountain of knowledge concerning the Chief, as the Scouts call him. Then I found out it was impossible to understand who he was until I understood the boys and the program." She smiled at Mr. Miles. "Scoutmaster Miles. I learned yesterday that Mr. Miles's interest started when he found out that a man he knew in his home town of Pampa, Texas, was a personal friend of Lord Baden-Powell. M.K. Brown not only knew the Boy Scout's founder, but he had a lot to do with convincing him to bring his new program to the United States. A wealthy man, Mr. Brown was very much a benefactor to Scouting. Is that not true, Mr. Miles?"

"It certainly is," the Scoutmaster chimed in. "He did a lot for Scouting in Pampa. He did a lot for the community in general."

"I had a lot of information Mr. Miles did not have," Eleanor continued. "But you can see he has returned the favor. I knew *what* B-P had done in his life, but I still did not know *who* he was. Though they had none of my facts and family information, and even though many of them barely know his name, the boys showed me who he was.

"Lord Baden-Powell was a decorated soldier and leader, a statesman, a spy, a recognized educator, and had a standing in his time that a sports super-star might have today. Yet it was pointed out to me that his tombstone bears none of that. His tombstone bears testimony of his love for Scouting, his love for these boys." She paused. "Girls too, of course. I certainly do not want to leave them out." Eleanor smiled at a young lady sitting with a family in the front row. "Originally they were called Girl Guides, but later the Girl Scouts became prominent, as well."

The young lady gave a smile and fidgeted in her seat.

"I envisioned B-P as I watched these boys. I saw him in my mind's eye at the age when school was such a trial for him. He loved going into the woods, camping, learning the skills that would serve him so well in the military, and which would later become the basis for the Scout program. I finally came to understand that the reason he was so sure the principles of Scouting could benefit a young man's life is because those same principles had helped shape his own life. He knew they could help shape the lives of others.

"I can also see the grown man here. I 'see' B-P standing behind the boys as they do each activity: his hands on his hips, campaign hat at a slight angle, smiling as he approves the things the boys are doing. I was surprised to see many activities being carried out by boys leading boys, rather than being led by the adult leaders. They told me that developing leadership traits is a main goal of the program. But there *is* always adult supervision. Every time the boys go out, the spirit of the Chief Scout is right there with them.

"I see tables without a father present. In some cases, he may be absent because of job responsibilities. But I imagine in many cases, a father's absence here today is due to the fact that many of you are single mothers. A very difficult job, I know. There are so many single-parent families these days. I am told that well over half of the families in this nation fall into that category. However, as fine a job as a single mother does—and I do not downplay this job in any manner—there is still a need for a strong male role model in a boy's life. B-P saw this need long ago, when he was training young soldiers. He decided this need should be addressed early in a boy's life. The Scout program intentionally puts fine role models in front of the boys. This is even more important today than it was during B-P's time."

Several of the mothers offered encouraging nods. Eleanor noted that a few had tears in their eyes.

"In many quarters today, I see a lack of respect growing in our young people. Respect was important to B-P. This week, I saw with my own eyes the respect and responsibility that is being generated among these young people here. To them, the twelve Scout laws are more than just words; they mean something together and individually." She looked at the Scouts with a smile. "Boys, can you repeat the laws for your parents and me?"

The boys came to their feet, gave the Scout sign, and spoke as one. "A Scout is trustworthy, loyal, helpful, friendly, courteous, kind, obedient, cheerful, thrifty, brave, clean, and reverent."

"Thank you, boys. You may be seated." As they sat, Eleanor continued. "Scoutmaster Miles gave a nice summary of each of the Scout laws when these young men said them last night. I will not attempt to do that here, but ask your sons. Ask them what each of the laws mean. These boys can tell you. The Scout laws are more than just words, and they will tell you that, as well."

Eleanor glanced over to where many of the boys were clustered. "Can you picture the Chief Scout of the World standing here as one of these boys?"

At first, most of the parents looked a little confused, but then they glanced toward the Scouts and nodded.

"I can too." The audience participation pleased Eleanor.

"Can you picture some of these boys going on to achieve the kind of international acclaim that he did?" Once again, she waited for the parents to respond, and they did.

"I can also picture that. If you look on the résumés of many business leaders, legislators, astronauts, sports figures, and even presidents, you will find that right along with education, awards, and achievements, these people mention they were Boy or Girl Scouts. Only four in a hundred Scouts are able to make it all the way to Eagle Scout. I assure you that if they *did* attain Eagle Scout, it is reflected on their résumés. You'll find it there for many who have achieved the most with their lives. Scouting lessons last a lifetime.

"I am writing a book on Lord Baden-Powell, but I came here and discovered that the real writing of the book is not with ink on paper, but it is written in the lives of boys and girls, and written far more eloquently. No book could possibly compare. I still intend to complete my project, but the version of B-P's life that sits right at the table with you says even more. That is a book with which you should be very familiar. One that is still being written, and one that you can have a profound impact on what the pages will say."

Eleanor looked at the crowd, unable to hide the tears that rose to cover her lashes. "Just make sure that the pages you help write in these young lives contain the same kind of respect and honor as the pages written by Lord Robert Baden-Powell, the Chief Scout of the World."

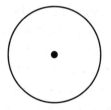

End of the Trail: This is the symbol the Boy
Scouts use to signify the end of a trail.

ONE HUNDRED YEARS OF SCOUTING

Dear Reader,

The upcoming anniversary, honoring one hundred years of Scouting, is a testimony to the success of Lord Baden-Powell and to celebrities, legislators, business leaders, astronauts, and even presidents who have been Eagle Scouts and who proudly list this achievement along with other major milestones in their lives. A lot of educational institutions seek to train young people in various aspects of their lives, but few seek to teach responsibility, honor, and respect. Few are able to provide a strong and meaningful male role model in so many lives that are sadly missing one.

There's something that happens to a young man who achieves that coveted Eagle rank, also to those who spend years in the program but who are unable to take it all the way. You can see it in their lives, can see it in the way they *approach* life. It changes them forever.

The legacy of Lord Baden-Powell is not found in the things he accomplished in his life, not even in the Scout organization he founded. But one hundred years later, his legacy is found in the lives of each Boy and Girl Scout who take the principles of Scouting to heart and who build their lives upon them. Boys and girls who put God and country first in their lives and understand the words "Be Prepared" acquire the skills that allow them to face problems with confidence.

Scouting is not just a *club*, but a way of life. That is the legacy of Lord Baden-Powell, spelled out one life at a time. May his legacy live on . . . one boy and girl at a time!

Eleanor Clark

THE SCOUTMASTER'S EASY CAMPFIRE RECIPES

These are *not* the recipes you will find in your mother's cookbook. The operational word here is *easy*. After all, we go camping to have fun, not slave over a hot stove . . . err . . . campfire. They aren't worded like cookbooks, but just the way guys teach other guys to cook on a campfire.

Disclaimer: Aluminum foil is one of the most important things in a Scout's kitchen, but get the *heavy-duty foil!* If the light foil is placed directly on the coals it will burn through.

Hot dog on a stick: This is probably the first one you need to get down. Most guys just cook it until it's black, then they know it's done. If you are a gourmet cook, you hold it higher over the fire until it looks like your big brother after he's been lying out on the beach too long. If you want to lessen the chance of dropping it into the fire or somebody knocking it off the stick during campfire swordfights, skewer it lengthwise. If you don't have chili, equal parts of ketchup and mustard work real well.

Making S'mores too much of a juggling act? There's an easy way. Roast a marshmallow and slap it between two fudge stripe cookies. That's a recipe even five-year-olds can get a handle on.

Bread on a Stick: Get a stick about an inch in diameter. Cover about 1-½ feet with foil, shiny side out. Grease the foil well, wrap canned crescent rolls around it and bake over the hot coals. Can also use biscuit mix. After mixing biscuits make a rope of the dough and wrap around stick leaving a little space between wraps. Serve with jam or honey.

A lot of cooking in Dutch ovens or even in foil is done on a little "nest" of coals pulled out of the fire for control. How do you judge how hot of a nest you have created? Here's a simple way: hold a hand, very cautiously, palm down over the coals. If you can hold it there 5 seconds it is low heat, 4 seconds medium, 3 seconds medium/high, and 2 seconds high. Usually there are twice the number of hot coals on the lid than beneath the pot for baking purposes.

Baked Potato in a Can: Clean a potato well, butter that sucker and season it, then drop it in a can and cover the top with foil. Set the can next to the coals of your fire for about 25 minutes, then without opening it up turn it 90 degrees and let it sit there for another 20 minutes. Pardner, that'll give you a first-class baked potato.

Omelet in a Bag: Use a good quality zip-lock type bag. Break 1 to 3 eggs into the bag; add a tablespoon of milk per egg, add cheese, bacon bits, peppers, onions, mushrooms or whatever you like in an omelet to the bag. Close the bag tightly, mash it all together, and drop bag into boiling water (water should be at a full boil). It will take 3 to 8 minutes, depending on how many bags are in the water. Can be thrown back into the water if you find yours isn't done enough.

Boiled Egg: Place egg in a hot cup (a paper one without the wax coating). Cover the egg with water and sit the cup on the coals. Have the seam on the cup away from the flames, as the cup may split open at the seam. Bring the water to a boil and boil for 10 minutes, adding more water as necessary to keep the egg covered. The cup will not catch fire as long as you make sure that there is enough water in the cup.

Hamburger Hobo Pie: Trust me, these guys know the easy way to cook a meal. Get a couple pounds of ground beef, slice up a big onion into good size chunks, do the same to a half dozen carrots, and cut a half dozen red potatoes into wedges. That's not hard, right?

Dust the whole thing good with seasoned salt and wrap it up in heavy aluminum foil. Set it next to the fire, but not right on the coals. About 30 minutes should get it done, turning it 90 degrees about half-way through. To be sure, you can cut a little slit in the foil with a knife and check the potatoes. When *they're* done, it's *all* done.

You can also cook this one on the way to your campout by wiring your foil pack to the manifold of the bus. An hour's driving time will get it done, but two cautions on this one. First, be really careful taking it off or you *will* get burned; and two, you're going to want to eat as soon as you get there—before setting up camp—because the smell of this one as you're going down the road will have you chewing on the seats before you arrive.

Here's a foil-cooking technique for **Meatloaf.** Cut a large onion stem to stern and hollow it out down to a couple of layers. Take some ground beef, add an egg, then add crackers or bread crumbs to get a nice meatloaf consistency. Spoon the meatloaf into the onion half and wrap it in foil. Cook it on a grille or next to the coals of the campfire about 20 minutes to a side (or next to the coals rotating 90 degrees after 20 minutes). This is another one that will work on the manifold of the bus with about a 45-minute driving time.

A similar thing can be done by cutting the top off a green pepper and stuffing it with the meatloaf—cooking it the same way to make a **Stuffed Pepper.**

Another way to do the ever-popular dog is called **Angels on Horseback**. Take you dog and slit it, putting cheese in the opening length-wise. Wrap the dog with bacon and stick it in place with toothpicks. Cook your dog over an open flame until the bacon is crisp, and you're set to go.

Getting the hang of it? Let's graduate to using those Dutch ovens. Now you're playing with the big boys. In the story we talked about "firing the pot" and getting them ready to cook. If you don't remember, go back and read that part again. It works the same no matter what we are going to cook. Here is the coolest secret of all. You can cook a one-pot meal. You learn the basic way to do it, and you vary it slightly depending on what your meat is. You're learning to cook a dozen different meals all at one time and people will think you are a major chef.

Let's start with **Beef Stew**. Put the Dutch oven on a nest of coals and brown three pounds of cubed beef (you can use hamburger if necessary). Cut up 6 or 8 medium potatoes into large chunks, slice up a half dozen carrots, and quarter a couple of nice-sized onions. If you have a can of green beans, they really help out. When the meat is brown, add a little water to produce some stock, then put the rest of the ingredients in. Put the lid on and put coals on the lid. Thirty minutes should get the potatoes done, but pull the lid with your pot hook and check them. When the potatoes are done it's ready. Salt and pepper individual portions to taste.

Want to do chicken instead? Substitute 6–8 chicken breasts. Instead of adding water to make stock, try using a very generous amount of Italian salad dressing. You'll put the same ingredients in and cook it the same way, but since the chicken needs to cook, plan on about an hour.

You can't order in **Pizza**, not if you are camping anywhere deserving of the name "camping." However, you can still have a deep-dish pizza. You just have to bring a couple of pizza crust mixes, Mozzarella cheese, and a little pizza sauce with you. Mix the crust mix per the package instructions and spread it in the bottom of your Dutch oven, bringing it up a half inch or so up the sides. Brush the dough with a little oil then spread a thin coat of pizza sauce over it. Brown a little hamburger or sausage and spread it on the pizza (pepperoni works well if you brought some). Add a little diced onion, and green pepper is nice if you have it. Place it on a smaller nest of coals than usual (don't want the bottom crust too brown) so you'll put most of the heat on the top. About 20–30 minutes will get it done.

Did you catch some *Fish*? Congratulations! Now you have them cleaned and filleted, so what do we do with them? Hopefully you were confident that you were going to catch something and you brought some lemon juice and butter, and maybe a little dill. Lay out that fillet on aluminum foil. Get a little pan and melt 3–4 tablespoons of butter. Put in a quarter cup of lemon juice, a teaspoon of salt, and dust it with black pepper. Slice some really thin onion pieces. Pour the mixture generously over the fish, cover it with the onion slices, then seal it tightly, but leave a little room for it to expand. Once again, cook it on a grille or on a nest of coals for 6–7 minutes per side. Yum.

The farmer down the way has ripe corn in his field! God does love Boy Scouts, doesn't he? I know you'll do it right and ask the farmer if your troop can have a dozen ears or so. He will, trust me. *Corn on the Cob* is easy to cook. Get those husks off and strip off all that corn silk. Cut the ears in half and put each on a piece of foil. We need to butter them liberally, and the way I like to do that is to spread a piece of bread thickly with butter. Use it to evenly spread butter on each ear, placing it on the foil (works with corn that is cooked, too). Sprinkle them with salt and pepper and seal them up. Put them on a nest of coals for about 15 minutes. You can do **Baked Potatoes** this way too, but you have to give them 30–45 minutes to be done.

Hot Dog Jubilee: You don't have to cook those dogs over the fire on sticks. Take 1 can of cherry pie filling and 1 package of hot dogs cut into chunks or a package of the little, bite-size dogs. Heat the pie filling over a campfire and stir in hot dogs. It makes a delicious sweet-and-sour hot dog dish.

Ready for a step up the dessert ladder? How about a **Dump Fruit Cobbler**? For this you need to bring along a couple of 16-oz cans of fruit pie filling and your favorite cake mix. Butter the inside of the Dutch oven and the bottom of the lid, then like the name says, just dump the cake mix and the filling into the pot. Pour a half cup water on top and set it on a nest of coals, putting more coals on the lid. It'll need to bake for 30–45 minutes, but test the cake to see if it is done.

Tuna Casserole: Here we mix two simple favorites, and as is so often true the sum of the whole is greater than its parts. Put on some macaroni to cook in a Dutch oven (you can use a couple of boxes of mac and cheese) and while the water is coming to a boil, you make some tuna salad. Put three large tablespoons of mayonnaise (I prefer Miracle Whip) into a bowl, add diced onion and a couple of table-spoons of sweet pickle relish. Add the tuna fish and mix it

159

well. That's a quick tuna salad and can be used separately for sandwiches.

For the casserole we drain the macaroni as soon as it is soft and stir the tuna salad into the pot with the macaroni. Layer the top with cheese slices and put the top of the Dutch oven on with some hot coals to bake for 10–15 minutes or until the cheese is melted. It's ready to go, and I like it with a side of pork and beans.

Do you have some tortillas with you? No, I'm not going to tell you how to make them from scratch. If you do, you can have **Breakfast Burritos**. You have to get the cast iron skillet dirty for this one. Put it on a nest of coals, then when it's hot, scramble some eggs, mixing in some chopped sausage and chopped onion (green pepper if you've got it). While it's cooking, in between occasionally stirring, use the heat from the skillet to warm the tortillas a few seconds on each side. Immediately butter one side. Fill the tortilla with the mixture, sprinkle on a little cheese, add a little salsa and chow down.

Another great thing to cook in a Dutch oven is **Baked Spaghetti**. To do this one you need to fire up the pot and cook a large onion diced, with a clove of garlic if you have it. Add a half pound of ground beef and cook it stirring occasionally. When cooked, add a can of tomato sauce and use that can to add two cans of water (getting every last bit of the tomato sauce). Cook for a few more minutes, then take a half pound of uncooked spaghetti and stir it in until it's well covered. Put the lid with hot coals on it and bake for an hour. Stir every 15 minutes. Add cheese on top and bake another 15 minutes, then you're good to go.

If you're having sandwiches, they don't need to be dull. How about making a *French Toasted Sandwich*? You make it just the way it sounds. Simply make a sandwich with the lunchmeat of your choice. Then dip the sandwich in milk, then flour, then egg, and finally drop it on a griddle. If you don't have a griddle, a heated Dutch oven works just fine. Brown and serve.

This also means you know how to make *French Toast*. You simply leave out the lunchmeat. Fix each piece of bread as above, dipping it in egg on both sides, brown them, dust with a little powdered sugar if you have it, pour on syrup and serve.

Speaking of not having a grille, a heated Dutch oven also works great for grilling *Hamburger Patties*. For a great tasting burger, having a little onion soup mix to add to the meat before making the patties is awesome.

Here's an easy but interesting one: *Coca-Cola Chicken*. Put 6–8 chicken breasts in an oiled Dutch oven. In a pot or bowl mix a can of Coke with a cup and a half of catsup, a teaspoon of garlic powder, one of onion powder, and two of chili powder. Spoon it over the chicken and bake it in the Dutch oven for an hour, spooning the pan juices over it every fifteen minutes. Ensure that chicken is done before serving.

Another really easy dessert is *Pudding in a Bag*. This simple treat takes instant pudding divided into zip lock bags. You simply add the appropriate amount of milk, seal, and mush with your fingers. In five minutes you have pudding that you can eat right out of the bag.

QUESTIONS AND REVIEW

Do you remember?

1. What merit badge did John, Samuel, and Alex earn?
2. What is the date of the founding of the Boy Scouts of America?
3. Identify the Scout song the boys sang around the campfire.
4. How many BSA 100th Anniversary silver dollars were minted?
5. Describe the "sneak attack."

Think about it:

1. List at least three reasons or events that led Lord Baden-Powell to start the Boy Scout movement.
2. Which character in the book would you like as a friend? What traits did this character show that you admire?

3. Choose six of the twelve Scout laws and give an example how you have demonstrated each of them.

Research Project:

Using the web links listed in the book, find information about three famous Eagle Scouts. How do you think attaining Eagle Scout helped them in their adult life?

Just for Fun:

Choose one of the recipes in the back of the book and prepare it at home. If possible, take it and share it at a BSA meeting.

Challenge:

In honor of the Boy Scouts of America's 100th anniversary, strive to recruit at least one new Scout member.

Earn:

Earn the Scouting Legacy Activity Badge by reading *The Legacy of Lord Baden-Powell,* answering the review questions, and recruiting a new Boy Scout member.

Scouting Legacy Activity Badge

GOD BLESS AMERICA

One of the most prolific songwriters in American history was Irving Berlin (1888–1989), and one of his most popular songs was "God Bless America." Mr. Berlin's generosity established the God Bless America Foundation in 1940, with all royalties from this patriotic song signed over to support and promote the nonsectarian work of the Boy Scouts and Girl Scouts. Composer Berlin's legacy lives on today in each Boy Scout and Girl Scout.

BOY SCOUT SILVER DOLLAR CENTENNIAL COMMEMORATIVE COIN

Silver Dollar Centennial Commemorative Coin
Honoring the 100th Anniversary
The Boy Scouts of America

O n October 8, 2008, President Bush signed into law the Boy Scouts of America Centennial Coin Act (HR 5872), which was introduced into Congress by Congressman Pete Sessions, who is an Eagle Scout. It had overwhelmingly passed in the House on April 22 and in the Senate on September 27. This bill recognizes the 100th anniversary of the Boy Scouts of America and authorizes 350,000 silver, one dollar coins to be minted in 2010. Each coin sold will include a $10 surcharge—representing a *$3,500,000 donation*—which will be made available to the National Boy Scouts of America Foundation to perpetuate the Scout legacy.

BOY SCOUT CENTENNIAL COMMEMORATIVE STAMP

To commemorate the centennial anniversary of the Boy Scouts of America, a Postage stamp was unveiled on November 13th, 2009, at the Smithsonian's National Postal museum, and will be released the summer of 2010. It will be dedicated to the Scouts during the 100th anniversary celebration at Ft. A. P. Hill, Virginia in July.

Representative Pete Sessions, R-Texas; Senator Dick Lugar, R-Indiana; Representative Ike Skelton, D-Missouri; and Senator Ben Nelson, D-Nebraska worked with the U.S. Postal Service to create the *Celebrate Scouting* stamp.

ABOUT THE AUTHOR

Eleanor Clark
Award-winning Author

While researching her family's rich American history, Eleanor conceived the idea for two series, *The Young Men of Honor Series* and *The Eleanor Series*.

Eleanor's passion for Scouting, history, and the appreciation of her American and Christian heritage comes to life in her novels. A mother, grandmother, and great-grandmother to Boy Scout members, Eleanor's first book in *The Young Men of Honor Series* is entitled *The Legacy of Lord Baden-Powell* and commemorates 100 years of Scouting in America.

The Eleanor Series won three national awards: *Eleanor Jo: A Christmas to Remember* won the 2008 National Indie

Excellent Award in Children's fiction and Melanie Ann: A Legacy of Love was awarded as a finalist. *Sara Jane: Liberty's Torch* took second place in the American Christian Fiction Writers YA 2008 Book of the Year Awards.

Eleanor lives in Texas with her husband of more than fifty-seven years and is devoted to their five children, seventeen grandchildren, and five great-grandchildren.

www.eleanorclark.com

KEY THINGS I LEARNED AT CAMP

_____

_____

_____

_____

_____

_____

_____

_____

_____

_____

_____

_____

_____

_____

_____

_____

_____

_____

_____

People from Camp I Want to Stay in Touch With

NAME	ADDRESS	CITY	STATE	ZIP CODE	E-MAIL ADDRESS

THE HISTORY OF SCOUTING:
WEB SITE LINKS

Some of the research for this book was done online. There is a wealth of information available for those who would like to pursue these links and follow them down the same trails as the author did:

Scouting

Boy Scout Trail—http://www.boyscouttrail.com/
Boy Scouts of America Homepage—http://www.scouting.org/
Catholic Scouting—www.catholicscouting-dallas.org
Circle 10 Council—http://www.circle10.org/site/c.owL1Kg
N4LxH/b.1455349/
England Scout Base—http://www.scoutbase.org.uk/
Jamboree—http://www.bsajamboree.org/
Life Saving Resources—http://www.lifesaving.com/
The Knot Page—http://www.earlham.edu/~peters/knotlink.
htm#knot%20tying
MacScouter—http://www.macscouter.com/

Merit Badge Center—http://www.meritbadge.com/

Order of the Arrow Home Site—http://www.oa-bsa.org/

Philmont Camp Site—http://www.philmont.com/page.php?page=site/home.php

Philmont page list—http://w4.lns.cornell.edu/~seb/philmont.html

Pinewood Pro scout links—http://www.pinewoodpro.com/links/scoutingresources.html

Pray Pub—http://www.praypub.org/main_frameset.htm

Ropers Knot Page—http://www.realknots.com/knots/index.htm

Scout Song—http://www.scoutsongs.com

Scout Store—http://www.boyscoutstore.com/

Scout Stuff (official catalog)—http://www.scoutstuff.org/bsasupply/

Scouter.com—http://www.scouter.com/

Scouters US Page—http://www.scouters.us/

Scoutorama—http://www.scoutorama.com/

Sourdough Bread—http://www.io.com/~sjohn/sour.htm

United Methodist Scouters—http://www.naums.org/

Western Star District page—http://www.westernstar.org/index.shtml

Woodbadge Scout leaders site—http://www.woodbadge.org/

Lord Baden-Powell

Baden-Powell Family History—http://www.pinetreeweb.com/bp-family-edgar-powell-891.htm

Lord Baden-Powell links—http://www.pinetreeweb.com/B-P.htm

Olive Baden-Powell (wife)—http://www.olavebadenpowell.org/

Pine Tree Web—http://www.pinetreeweb.com
Robert Baden-Powell as an educator—http://www.infed.org/thinkers/et-bp.htm
http://www.eleanorseries.com
http://www.youngmenofhonorseries

SOURCES

Baden-Powell, Lord Robert, *Lessons from the Varsity of Life*, Pine Tree Web. http://www.pinetreeweb.com/bp-vars.htm.

West, James E. "Our Fifth World Jamboree." Pine Tree Web.http//www.pinetreeweb.com/1937-wj5-west-article.htm.